Mishap
Or
Design

Dr. J. Oliver Johnson

Negative
Imprint

For Julian

ONE

Banjo Larry's eyes snap open as a dog and its owner jog past him, the dark brown Labrador's leash hanging limp between his neck and his owner's hand. They run in unison, the dog and the young woman, and they appear to be in no hurry at all, as if the activity is a routine occurrence. It is routine, in fact, and Banjo Larry knows this, as he has awoken to the same athletic pair several times from this and various other benches at the expansive city park. They are but a few beings who jointly inhabit this common place routinely from time to time.

The emergence of other people there and the sounds they make in their activities not only allows Larry to awaken to the new day, but also signifies his time to depart. The local police force, though not very prominent there in those morning hours, will sometimes still harass the vagrants early in the day.

Still clutching his guitar tight against his chest, he sits up straight and stands. His pillow, which is a dirty red canvas backpack during the non-sleeping hours, falls into its proper place, having been strapped to the man's back even while he slept. Everything he possesses in life — including leftovers from his previous existence — is in that ever-present red bag, save the worn-out clothes on his back and the guitar held by its neck in Larry's left hand.

As he stands, ready to face the dawn, he slides a dirty old fedora from over his eyes to the top of his head, covering most of his ratty mop of brown hair and helping to cast a shadow over the three-day-old stubble on his neck and face. That hair, which was silky and clean just a few days ago, looks right at home under the old hat, which is crusty and well-worn after many years spent shielding the outside elements from the wearer, who, until just last night, had been someone else entirely.

The human creatures here are of all types, some homeless who find refuge in the park's serenity and some who only show up to take advantage of the jogging paths or picnic areas.

Larry spots a man who is not entirely unfamiliar to him, though he can't recall ever hearing the man's preferred name even after three or so years of occupying the same general space as him at various times.

That man, who appears to be in his mid-thirties, is riding on a shiny ten-speed bicycle, a large bag of recyclable materials tied to each side of the handlebars. He's a simple man — his intelligence level no higher than that of a young grade-schooler — who is kind enough until provoked by someone who knows just what to say to instigate a fistfight with the poor guy. He's straddling his bike as Banjo Larry passes him, leaning into a trash can and digging out any empty bottles and cans he can find. After his bags are unable to hold any more, he'll ride his bike back home to his mother. Larry smiles and offers a nod to the man as he strolls by and receives a smile and a friendly wave in return.

Several yards up the walking path, Larry steps aside at the sight of an oncoming jogger, who is about as known to him as the recycler is. Anybody who has ever encountered this particular runner knows better than to play chicken with him, as the man would sooner plow into you than to swerve out of your way. And just as anybody who knows of him would do in this situation, Larry greets the wild-eyed shirtless man and the runner obliges him with the usual karate-style kick into space before resuming his exercise.

Upon coming to a free-standing water fountain, Larry removes a plastic water bottle from his red backpack and fills it to the brim, drinks his fill from it, fills it again and screws the cap back on tightly — a simple action made somewhat difficult by the bandages on his hands — before returning the bottle to his bag. By the time he has followed the cement walkway to the street, he has dug through his pockets and retrieved a small handful of loose change, which he uses to buy a candy bar from a newspaper stand.

He takes his time eating this breakfast as he continues down the sidewalk along the busy city street. Unlike many people there, Larry makes sure to hold onto his empty candy bar wrapper until he comes to a trash can. Those who sleep on the streets know the importance of keeping them clean and are actually less likely to carelessly litter than the more "civilized" individuals who drive to this area in fancy cars, wearing pleated pants and drinking four-dollar cups of coffee.

There are many other street people along Larry's walk, some more obviously so than others. Some of these people ignore everyone who passes, some will offer a smile or maybe a pathetic stare in hopes of a coin or two landing on the pavement in front of them, and some even greet Banjo Larry by name as he passes them. A few of these people have lived outside for most of their lives, while some are relatively new to this type of living, victims of either uncontrollable circumstance or poor decisions. For Larry, it's maybe a mixture of both, having found himself accidentally outdoors a while ago but failing to jump at the occasional chances presented to him that would have brought back a much more comfortable existence inside.

After about an hour and a half of casual but brisk walking, Banjo Larry finally nears his destination, which, in a way, was sort of his starting place long ago. It was here, after all, where he first mistakenly became a man without a permanent address, a tired soul destined to roam the streets, seeking the occasional roof over his head, but — for reasons known only to that lonely wanderer — denying himself the few opportunities that arose from time to time for permanent shelter.

He finds himself at the beach — or standing in a small parking lot adjacent to it, rather. There is but one empty parking space in the entire lot, the rest having been already occupied by the vehicles of tourists and lazy beachgoers, some of them no doubt playing hooky from their jobs or schools. This is, after all, a weekday, which means nothing to Larry now, though it would have been a factor in his daily activities had he still been living his previous life.

Standing in that one empty parking space watching the tide, Larry can't help but feel that the spot was left vacant for him, though he does not have an automobile to park there. Before — well, that was an entirely different story altogether, because, as it were, he had parked a car here once, in this very parking space. But now, a lifetime later, all he can do is stand here and admire from the spot the endless blue ocean, wondering, remembering....

SNAP!

Larry is thrust from his daydream as his head whips around in an involuntary reaction to the car horn blasting him from behind. Even before his entire body completes a full spin to the rear, he sees the shiny grill of a new luxury automobile, metallic silver and chrome. A fine car, indeed, and Larry is standing between it and its rightful place. With a smile and an apologetic wave, Banjo Larry scurries out of the way and the vehicle pulls into what was the last open space.

"That's a beautiful car," Larry says, and he's a man who knows what a beautiful car looks like.

"Isn't it, though?" The man returns, clearly a business-type who reeks of self-importance and an over-inflated salary. This is also something Larry knows firsthand about.

"Yes, sir, it sure is."

"You'll make sure nothing happens to it, right?"

"I sure will, sir." Banjo Larry is not above kissing up to snobs anymore, but only for the possibility of small monetary compensation. It's a survival tactic taught to Larry by a wise, old friend of his.

This jerk in the BMW, for example, thanks the poor hobo for his admiration with three folded dollar bills before strutting around to the passenger side of the car, where he opens the door for his female companion, who seems just as egotistical as the driver. Larry stuffs the money into the front right pocket of his dusty blue jeans. This cash, he knows, will buy his next meal, which will hopefully be a little more than a simple candy bar.

Lunch will have to wait, and possibly be dinner instead. It's always a good idea to space your meals out, Larry has learned, since you can never know when you'll have enough change to buy that next bit of food.

For now, Larry is making his way onto the beach, heading out to where the tide meets the warm sand. He's got something to take care of that he's been putting off for far too long.

TWO

Though it's easy to see where someone is, their position in life is not completely understood until you know where they previously were. And even then, it's not until you can fully appreciate how they got to being from where they were to where they currently are that you are able to empathize, sympathize or even care about that person and the predicament in which they find themselves.

You see, Banjo Larry the homeless guitar player wasn't always so. In fact, he had a childhood and an upbringing probably quite similar to your own. Well, maybe the very beginning of his story differs from most, but it had no real bearing on the rest of his story.

His biological parents were related to him by nothing more than the blood they shared. His father had been confined to a prison cell since before the birth of his boy, eventually dying there some years later without having any real knowledge that he had even fathered a child. The teenage mother, whose life could be described as turbulent at best, gave up her addictions when faced with the pregnancy. Unfortunately, just days after the birth, she resumed her habits and overdosed on something much more powerful than her body was able to stand before she'd entered her period of sobriety.

After her death, the infant was put up for adoption and taken in by a loving couple who could bear no children of their own. And it was these parents who provided for the child what any loving family would, as they were secure and comfortable in both financial and emotional terms.

The child, who was rechristened Fabian upon his adoption, had a clean slate on which he could etch out a promising future, and he did. Like any other intelligent lad with the means to do so, young Fabian excelled in school and earned a college degree. He was always gainfully employed after that and took a local beauty, Tracy, for a wife. And it was she who bore Fabian a child, a seemingly healthy son they named Ellis, after the father Fabian so admired.

And like any other average family in America, this family had a home with a yard, two cars in their driveway and a warm meal to share each night before they retired to their cozy beds.

But now, almost a decade later, Fabian finds

himself staring into the depths of the Pacific Ocean, with an entirely different past to remember and an equally different moniker with which he must live with these pasts. No straight line, it seems, could ever be able to trace out how this man got from where he was to where he is.

Where Banjo Larry is, exactly, is Santa Cruz, California, not too far from its renowned boardwalk. And while folks in his situation actually do live here, most others at the beach are simply visitors, tourists looking for relaxation, maybe fun, and a peaceful setting for reflection. Larry was once one of these people, but that was toward the final stages of his life as a man known by the name of Fabian.

As Banjo Larry still remembers so vividly to this day, Fabian — a clean-cut, handsome man in his very early thirties on that final day of the rest of his life — steps out from his tiny apartment dwelling for the last time, though he does not know at the time that it will be his final exit from the home he has shared with nobody but his demons for but a few long weeks.

Draped over one arm is a garment bag, just recently zipped shut with a nice suit, tie and shoes inside. Currently, he's wearing a bright white polo shirt, a pair of crisply starched blue jeans and a pair of running shoes that appear to have never been run in before. He will need that other outfit — the more professional one — later in the day, and he will change into it once he reaches San

Francisco, the last of today's destinations, where he will deliver to a building there most of the contents of a bright red backpack before returning home to his apartment. The backpack is slung over both shoulders. He hasn't been accustomed to wearing a backpack since his school days, but he will soon get used to it once again.

Stepping out in the early morning hours before even the sun has forced itself to welcome the new day, Fabian gently sets his garment bag and backpack in the back seat of his white Mercedes-Benz, next to a child's car seat that will remain forever without an occupant. Fabian knows the booster seat sits there without a purpose anymore, but he hasn't found it in his heart to throw it out just yet.

Also on Fabian's agenda is a quick visit to the beach in Santa Cruz, a place he has visited several times in the past with Tracy and Ellis and where he plans to make his first deposit of the day from the contents of that red backpack.

After an uneventful drive along the California freeway, Fabian finally arrives within the city limits and he makes his way toward the beach, passing a man who appears to be homeless, wearing camouflaged pants and holding a sign that reads VETERAN — GOD BLESS.

Fabian pays the man no attention and steers his car into a parking lot next to the sand. The small lot is almost completely empty as it is still relatively early in the day, and Fabian picks a spot facing the ocean and parks the vehicle.

Leaving his bags in the back seat of the car, Fabian steps out onto the sand and makes his way toward the tide. His plan is to reminisce for a short while of happier times, back when he visited this same spot with Tracy and Ellis before either one of his loved ones showed any signs of illness.

He finds a comfortable looking spot in the sand, far away from the few people already out there this early on a Wednesday morning. As his mind wanders to nonspecific dates behind him, the tide washes in and out, at some times with more strength than at others, but never coming even remotely close enough to threaten Fabian with a cold rinsing.

He can remember Ellis's voice here, in something of a dream within a dream, as the boy proclaimed his desire to stay here forever, his youth and innocence itself a thing of beauty. Yes, if Ellis had his way, he would have stayed on that beach and in that blue water for all of eternity, and Fabian hopes to, in a way, make that happen. Tracy also seemed to be at her happiest at that beach, but her mood was always dependent on the happiness of her only son. As long as Ellis could be happy there forever, Fabian knows that Tracy would be, as well.

Ellis loved the sand the most, even more than he loved the water, and he especially loved to build castles in the warm sand. And though he was small and young, he was always determined to build what in his eyes was a grand fortress, complete with a moat full of imaginary alligators to keep out any bad guys who may invade.

"Here, baby," Tracy would always say to Ellis. "Let me help you with that." And the two of them could sit for hours, just piling sand upon sand, Ellis smiling and Tracy staring lovingly into the eyes of her precious little boy. Neither one of them cared that soon after completion, every sandcastle they ever built would be knocked down flat by an uncaring wave.

As Fabian's happiest memories are relived through his daydreaming, the area is slowly filling with visitors and the tide is but a few inches from the man's feet. Before long, a bigger wave ferociously rolls in, sending an unexpectedly large tide up to the beach to soak Fabian's jeans up to the knees.

As he stands, wet and cold, he remembers the time Ellis dumped an entire bucket of water onto him. He had then picked the laughing boy up into the air, set him on his shoulders and marched directly into the ocean. Not the least bit scared, Ellis demanded his father take him deeper, deeper into the water. And so they went, until Ellis's feet barely skimmed the top of the water and Fabian hyperventilated slightly as the cold water of the Pacific surrounded his chest.

"Not too far," Tracy warned, somewhat

concerned about Fabian's ability to keep her son from going under.

"Tell her it's okay," Fabian urged the boy, who waved at his mother while she snapped a few photos of the happy father-son duo from dry land.

The flash from Tracy's camera — or the memory of it, rather — awakens Fabian from his standing daydream, though his current reality is only a blur through the salty tears welling up in his eyes and rolling steadily down his suntanned cheeks to his lips. With the same drive he had marched into that water before, he does so again, past the splashing children and their curious parents, without concern for his personal safety or future comfort once he emerges in dripping wet duds.

Once the waves are slamming hard against his chest, much harder than he had allowed them to get while carrying Ellis on his shoulders, Fabian turns around to face the beach. But instead of his beautiful wife and her camera staring back at him, it's now the faces of confused onlookers, wondering why a fully-clothed man in long pants and shoes would suddenly storm off the beach. Pointing and gawking, dozens more join in the viewing.

Confused, embarrassed, still grieving for his family, Fabian sees no point in returning to dry land. Instead of facing those spectators — and the rest of his life, in general — he turns around once more and continues marching deeper, deeper into the freezing ocean until he is knocked down by a giant wave. His automatic response, whether voluntary or not, is to stand and grasp for air, but the subsequent waves prevent him from doing this.

Fabian is thrown around like a single wet towel in a clothes drier, tumbling and twisting as he's pulled out to sea, and he quickly loses consciousness.

THREE

Fabian awakens abruptly in the water near the beach, but not the same stretch of beach he last remembers standing on.

He's choking, coughing, grasping for any breath of air he can get a hold of, fresh or otherwise. Two surfers — one a man in his early twenties and another just a bit older than his buddy — are dragging Fabian in on the back of a surfboard. They toss him onto the dry sand and kneel over him, one of them readying himself to perform the mouth-to-mouth portion of CPR on their recent catch. In the nick of time, as far as the two lifesavers are concerned, Fabian spits out a lungful of saltwater, signifying it is no longer necessary to attempt resuscitation procedures.

This section of beach, though technically along the same California coastline as where he went under, is much more isolated as large masses of gray rock extend from the water to far into the land, making it less accessible to those wandering in from the street. Nowhere is the crowd of people staring in wonder at what must have appeared to be either drunken or simply suicidal actions on Fabian's part. Gone are the beach chairs and umbrellas, sand castles and Frisbees. There is only Fabian here, and two stereotypical-looking west coast surfers.

"You should've just let me drown," Fabian mutters between spouts of vomiting and gasps for air.

"I've got a cell phone in the van," one guy excitedly proclaims. "I'm gonna go call 911."

"No!" Fabian is on his belly now, trying desperately to pick himself up. "I'm alright. I don't need an ambulance."

They help Fabian sit up, then sit back, watching to ensure the tired man is alright.

"Where am I?"

"You're in Santa Cruz now, dude. That's in California," the younger man tells him, as if he's speaking to an extraterrestrial that just crash-landed on Earth. "Did you fall off a fishing boat someplace?"

"No, I fell off the beach someplace."

Fabian, now having regained his breath and some of his composure, stands up fully and his two rescuers follow him up.

"I need to get back to my car," Fabian says quite calmly, considering the circumstances of the events that brought him there in the first place. "Do you have any idea which way the parking lot is?"

"I don't know, man," the older of the two says, "but judging by the direction of the current and the waves, I'd say you came from that direction." He extends his pointer finger, with its raison-like skin, in the most likely direction.

"Good. I have money in my car. I'll give you some of it for saving my life."

"No, that's alright, dude," the younger one says generously. "It was no problem at all. We just wanted to make sure you were alright."

Fabian insists they take some money as a token of his gratitude, but they again decline.

"There's a road just over that sand ridge there," the older gentleman tells him. "You catch that road and you can follow it back to your car, for sure."

Fabian thanks the men again and stumbles through the sand toward the road, and hopefully back to his car that he now decides will take him home immediately. The trip to San Francisco will have to wait until later, tomorrow at the earliest. He's soaking wet and completely filthy. He can feel sand and dirt rubbing into the skin over his entire body.

Upon reaching the sidewalk, he follows it in the general direction he was advised to travel, limping and coughing past the occasional homeless person sitting pitifully on the sidewalk.

Few even look up to make eye contact with him. One man holds out his hand for a possible offering of spare change, but he withdraws his arm when he gets a look at Fabian, who appears to the bum to be worse off than himself.

It is nighttime when Fabian finally reaches the familiar parking lot and he quickly finds his car, even as the area has reached its full capacity of vehicles.

He is initially relieved to find that his belongings — the garment bag and the red backpack — are still inside and his car appears to be in the same condition as when he left it. His relief quickly turns to frustration upon the realization that his pockets are completely empty of their previous contents, replaced now by sand and grime. His wallet and keys are now somewhere on the ocean's floor and he knows he has no chance at ever recovering them.

With the evening's darkness quickly enveloping him and the lack of anybody within sight of his car, Fabian makes the decision to break a window and retrieve his belongings. A window, he figures, could always be replaced. He'll make a phone call tomorrow morning and have a new one installed before lunchtime. Also, a locksmith's services will be in order as the only other spare key to the Mercedes sits in a junk drawer near the one containing the silverware back at his apartment.

He looks around for a blunt object of some

kind, cannot immediately find one and decides to break through with his fist.

No, he says to himself, *a swift kick would hurt much less*, before abandoning that idea altogether and searching once again for a makeshift tool. About ten feet away from the front of the car, next to a trash can, he finds it. The jagged chunk of blacktop must be leftover remnants from the last time this parking lot was torn up and rebuilt.

With a single blow, Fabian crashes the chunk through the rear driver-side door window, sending tiny pieces of automobile glass clear across to the other side of the interior, some even settling into Ellis's seat.

Quickly, before anybody has a chance to investigate the destructive sound they may have heard, Fabian opens the door, grabs his two bags from the back seat, then scurries out of the parking lot and into the glow of the city street lights. He'll come back in the morning, he figures, after he's gotten some well-deserved sleep and a hot shower in the first hotel he comes to.

He could call someone tonight, either the police department or his insurance company, but it'll take hours for him to verify to them that he is indeed who he must claim to be in order to get his car driving once again, and he just doesn't have it in him to stay awake any longer than he absolutely has to.

Fabian passes by a sandwich shop. It's closed, and that's too bad because Fabian is starving. He comes to a Chinese food restaurant that is still open, but it is now that he realizes that even as hungry as he may be right now, his feeling of exhaustion is so much more overpowering. The aromas billowing out from the open door are almost enough to make him stop for a quick meal, but he perseveres nonetheless. He must make it to a hotel, the sooner the better. Any undue delay may mean his crashing down onto the pavement below his soggy, blistered feet — not a product of conscious decision-making, of course, but of the simple fact that this well-to-do man has never before had his body worked over in a month's worth of gym visits as he's had during the course of just today's happenings.

Finally, he sees it: a hotel, a motel — he can't be sure which from this far away. According to the lit letters of the giant sign, it may simply be an *otel.* Either way, he is sure it has beds for rent and running water, which is all he requires tonight. He can rough it as well as any man, he tells himself.

"I'm going to need to see a driver's license or another form of government-issued picture ID, sir," the effeminate middle-aged man behind the counter sneers when Fabian asks for a room.

"I'm really sorry," Fabian explains, "but I lost my wallet in the ocean and I don't have any identification on me right now."

"Lost your wallet, huh?" as if Fabian's trying to pull some sort of scam on him. "So that means you also don't have any major credit cards on your person, I take it?"

"No credit cards, sorry, but I can pay by cash." Fabian removes his backpack, opens it up and pulls out a bundle of twenty-dollar bills.

"I'm sorry, sir, but our policy clearly states that you need a government-issued form of identification to rent a room here."

His occupation as the nighttime desk clerk at this seedy otel clearly puts this man in a sort of position of authority he would otherwise never find himself in.

As his tired knees fight the urge to buckle below him, Fabian knows he's in no condition or mood to walk away in search of another place to sleep for the night. If he must pay five-star prices for a room in an establishment that should probably be condemned, so be it.

"Sir, I understand your policy," Fabian pleads desperately, "and I'm begging you to let me rent a room here tonight. I've had a long and terrible day and I just need a place to sleep. I can more than pay for the room, plus throw in something extra to show my appreciation for you being so kind and understanding to my dire situation."

"Like I said, we have policies in place that cannot simply be ignored whenever I fancy," he countered. "Besides, bribery is illegal and you're lucky I don't call the cops right now. And on top of that, your money looks fake and your personal hygiene is highly suspect. Now please leave this place of business before I'm left with no other choice but to call the police and have you removed by force."

Knowing that there is nothing between here and where he left his car, Fabian continues on down the road but never does find what he is looking for. The sidewalk he's on eventually forks and, in his state of delirium brought on by dehydration and extreme exhaustion, he follows the side that leads into a public city park instead of the one that separates the park from the quiet but well lit main street. As he realizes his mistake, he also comes to the realization that he has walked at least eight miles now, possibly ten, from the parking lot.

The parking lot? Yes, the parking lot! He could sleep in his car for the night. Broken window or not, the seat of a Mercedes-Benz sure beats a cement park bench, of that much he is certain. But it's so far away.

If it comes to it, he'll sleep in the car tomorrow night. There is simply no possible way he can make it back there tonight. His mind has been wandering just as much as his body has all along this death march, and he doesn't know how much longer he can tolerate the stress-induced hallucinations. No longer considering himself a religious man as of late, Fabian does think of Moses right now and stops short of comparing tonight's activities to the biblical man's forty-year walk through the desert. *At least Moses had followers,* Fabian says to himself. *The only one behind me is my own shadow on the ground.*

A bench is his bed for the night, the canopy of trees his roof. Feeling uncomfortable and overexposed in the public park, Fabian silently fears for his own personal safety and the security of his possessions. Clutching his garment bag tightly against his chest, he lies on his back, sliding the red backpack high below his head as he closes his eyes while the cool Pacific breeze dances with the warmth of the still night.

You'll have to kill me first if you're gonna steal from me, he says to himself.

"Go ahead," he mumbles aloud. "Come on over and kill me."

FOUR

Again, Fabian's thoughts have involuntarily drifted back to the not-so-distant past — a little more than five years ago now — to the year of the great flood. It was a flood like many others, actually, in the farming region along the San Joaquin River, a very minor occurrence just about every year and a slightly major one less frequently, only in those years of excessive but much needed rainfall. This particular flood, however, is great in significance because of its correlation to other life events that spun on that same axis in time and space. This was to become a major turning point in Fabian's life. He knew this, of course, but he did not yet know the full details or the extent of the impact.

These thoughts of his, vivid more now than they were earlier on the beach, come presently during time of actual slumber, and far deep does this man sleep tonight, no longer able to feel the discomfort of the thick concrete slab that is a park bench beneath him, nor is he able now to stir himself from the dream when the surrealism of it, whether good or ill, is more than his poor mind can tolerate.

The roads were flooded during that time more than half a decade — and seemingly a lifetime — ago. For fear of being washed off of the road and into a watery grave, Fabian drove slowly and carefully. Under these circumstances, one normally does drive in this manner. But there were other circumstances facing Fabian — or lying directly behind him, rather, in the back seat — that would entice a man in drier weather to speed down the road like a madman.

The telephone was nonfunctional at their home as a result of the heavy rainfall, and Tracy was in the final stages of her first pregnancy, and they were scared. The couple had no other choice than to make their own way to the hospital. Fabian considered himself to be very proficient in many areas. In childbirth, however, he had no experience at all.

The car slammed to a halt in front of the hospital's entrance, and Tracy moaned loudly with the rocking of the car.

"Sorry, baby," Fabian said, looking over to her from the front seat. "Are you alright?"

"Yes!" she screamed. "Just get me outta here!"

They were safe in the hospital just seconds

later, and regardless of what was happening outside, it would no longer affect the delivery of Fabian and Tracy's first child, a boy they had already decided to name Ellis, which was a family name. Other factors, however, were also involved, and they did have such an effect.

After a few hours of what Fabian expected were normal childbirth procedures, the delivery room suddenly filled with the sounds of various beep, buzzes and rings. Doctors and nurses rushed in, others rushed out, but then rushed back in again. From Fabian's perspective, the room began to spin.

"You're gonna need to step outside," one short but powerful nurse told Fabian as she forced him out the door. "Don't worry; we'll take care of her."

It was another hour, maybe more, before Fabian heard any news regarding what had just happened and of the condition of his wife and child.

"Mr. Grunauer," Fabian heard the doctor say. "It looks like there's been a premature closure of the fetal ductus arteriosus."

"I don't know what that means," Fabian cried. "What does that mean? Is she alright?"

The doctor motioned for Fabian to sit in one of the chairs positioned along the wall, and the two sat.

"What that essentially means, if this is what happened, is that the baby was denied an acceptable amount of oxygen, which resulted in fetal distress."

"Fetal distress?" What the hell did that even mean?

"Yes, fetal distress," the doctor continued. "We needed to perform emergency surgery to get the baby out as soon as possible. Your son was delivered by Caesarean section."

"And he's okay?"

"Yes, Fabian, he's fine."

"And my wife?" Fabian almost screamed. "What about my wife?"

"During the initial surgery," the doctor explained, "the surgeon noticed placenta accreta, which is an abnormal superficial attachment of the placenta to the myometrium."

"What does *that* mean?"

"That's the middle layer of the uterine wall."

"I still don't understand what you're talking about."

"It means she required another surgery to stem the bleeding and fully remove the placenta."

"Is she alright?" Fabian demanded. "Is that bad?"

"She'll probably need a hysterectomy. It looks like she'll be alright, but she'll most likely never be able to have any more children."

FIVE

Fabian awakens early, much earlier than he usually does but understandably early this morning considering it's happening on a park bench for the first time in his life. A coat of fresh dew covers his entire face and the garment bag he still clutches tightly against his chest.

He sits up on the seat, his red backpack sliding low on his back with its straps still slung over his shoulders. He's somewhat amazed by the fact that he was neither mugged nor murdered in his sleep last night.

He's still tired, and if he felt this way at home, he'd simply pull the covers up over his head and pass out once again.

Fabian tries to assess his situation, find out exactly where he is in relation to where he needs to be. His car is miles away, but it's his only means of returning to life as he knows it — as dreadful as it may have become for him recently — back in his tiny apartment.

A shower will have to wait until later today, and San Francisco will have to wait for another outing completely. His clothes are now dry, the sand between the fabric and his skin much more bearable, though Fabian knows he will never admit this sense of physical comfort he feels in comparison to yesterday's torture.

Walking to the street, he tries to remember how far away the Chinese food place was, its aroma still appealing. His hunger today is stronger than he has ever experienced it before. He'll find food on his way to that loathsome parking lot, as well as a place to use the restroom and wash up as best as he could before eating. He's still covered with a thin layer of grime. He's not quite sure what it is, but it can't be all too healthy for him if it's ingested.

In the corner of his eye he spots what appears to be a public restroom. Yes, it is, and he has never in his life been more relieved to have a chance to use such facilities. It's made of brick, or concrete block, that has been painted a bland white, probably to cover the spots of graffiti left by some common hoodlums.

It needs another coat of white, Fabian notices, to hide the damages left recently, possibly even last night as he slept nearby.

There's no soap in the dispenser or paper towels in the holder, but he does his best to make himself as presentable for public viewing as reasonably possible under these conditions.

The Chinese food place is still closed as he passes it — *of course it is, damn it* — and so Fabian keeps on walking. Plan B, he calculates in his head without breaking from his quick stride, is to suffer through the hunger for the time being. His stomach, completely hollow now, should soon start to turn on itself and the pain should subside. First, he'll recover his car and call a locksmith, who will need to be paid in cash, obviously, since the fate of Fabian's wallet keeps it about as far out of reach as his spare key in the drawer. Somewhere along his drive back home, he will stop in to one of those greasy fast food drive-thru restaurants. It's not his preferred meal, but at least that way he can also avoid any interaction with other diners, which is something he's sure they'd appreciate.

The parking lot is once again packed, but his car is nowhere in sight. At first, Fabian is angry. He must've somehow taken a wrong turn and ended up at another lot, but then his frustration grows further upon his finding the chunk of concrete from last night and the bits of broken window glass.

Across the street, Fabian notices a uniformed policeman and he makes his way toward the officer.

"Excuse me, officer," Fabian begins. "I was wondering if you could help me out. My car was stolen sometime last night from that parking lot over there. It's a white Mercedes-Benz."

"White Mercedes-Benz, huh?" The cop leers at Fabian suspiciously. "Well, if that really was your car, it was towed this morning. Vandalized, ticketed last night, then they came in this morning and towed it away. You can't park your car there overnight like that."

"Yeah, I lost my keys. How can I get it back?"

"There should be a sign over there with a phone number to the impound yard," the policeman explains. "You give 'em a call and they'll tell you where the yard is. Go down there, show your ID, pay the fine — if you can afford it — and they'll give you your car back. But, like I said, that's only if it's really your car."

Fabian explains to the nice officer how he lost his wallet yesterday, along with his keys, in the ocean. He'll be able to get a new driver's license, he assures the cop, but it will take some time, and he must have his car in order to make it happen.

"You know it's illegal to be walking around out here in public without an ID card, don't ya?" The cop lets Fabian know that he's obviously misjudged the level of this public servant's sincerity. "It's also illegal to jaywalk like you just did. You keep pestering me about this sort of crap and I might just take you down to the jailhouse for the night. But you'd like that, wouldn't you? Three hot meals and a roof over your head? Play your cards right, and you might even get a warm shower thrown into the deal."

"But I'm not homeless, sir."

"You really feel like testing me?"

"No, sir." And Fabian was once again on his way. Now is when he realizes that he may be stuck in town for a little while longer than he had hoped.

Approaching a drugstore, the tired wanderer decides to stop in and purchase a pen and small notepad. He'll need them to take down the information from the sign so he can get his car back. He also buys a toothbrush, a small tube of toothpaste, antibacterial hand sanitizer and a bar of soap. Somehow, he's convinced himself, he will get a hotel room before tonight.

Not far up the road, in the direction he wishes he had taken last night, is a diner. The outside of the building places it right at home in this city, but inside it looks more like something from an old Norman Rockwell painting. He sets his garment bag down in a booth and carries his shopping bag of recently acquired items into the restroom at the rear of the restaurant. In there, Fabian washes his face and arms at the sink, then brushes his teeth. *I really should've brought in my suit to change into,* he says to himself. Regardless, he really should've known better than to leave it sitting there alone at the table. *If someone needs it bad enough to steal it from me, then they can have it.*

When he returns to the booth, his bag is still there, along with a hot cup of coffee. Fabian sits down and picks up the menu lying next to the steaming cup. The waitress — a thin but attractive girl right around his age — makes her way over to him just as the newspaper delivery guy comes in with a bundle of papers.

"Do you need some more time with the menu?" she asks politely and routinely-sounding.

Handing her the menu without ever having looked it over, he orders a short stack of pancakes and scrambled eggs to go with his coffee, and one of today's newspapers, if it's not too much trouble.

She flips open her notebook and quickly jots down the order. Taped to the front cover of her notepad is a photograph of a young boy — probably her son, Fabian figures.

"Is that your kid?"

She flips the pad closed and turns it over to look at it herself. As she does, Fabian can see a gleam of light turn on in her tired eyes as she looks upon the image of her preschool-aged child.

"Enjoy him while you can," he tells her as he takes a sip of coffee.

"Yeah, because he'll be all grown up someday."

"Yeah." Sometimes, Fabian knows, they don't grow up at all.

"Well, between this job and my other one, and then the night school, there isn't much time for just the two of us."

"I don't mean to stick my nose in anybody else's business, miss," Fabian starts cautiously, "but you really ought to take some time off to spend with him before it's too late."

"I hear ya, but that's easier said than done," she counters politely. "I'll go put your order in with the cook."

She smiles at him again when she brings his food, trying her best to pretend it's a wonderful day but still looking tired and worn out and obviously hating to be there while her son is elsewhere. Fabian eats his breakfast while flipping through the newspaper sporadically. He turns back to the front page just as the waitress takes away his empty plates and refills his coffee cup. He thanks her again and sips more hot coffee as he glances to the headline of a short story near the bottom right corner of the front page:

Man wades into tide, disappears

Fabian follows along to the story that most readers might simply breeze past. To this reader, however, the topic appears personal as an unidentified San Joaquin County man reportedly walked out into the current yesterday morning and was washed away by the tide. A car, identified by police as belonging to a person fitting the presumably-drowned man's general description, was found parked in a nearby lot. The identity of the man is being withheld pending notification of his family, and the public is asked that any information they have in the matter be reported to police as their investigation continues.

Divers will search the waters later today, the paper reports, but investigators are quoted as saying that in most drowning cases this close to shore, the body is usually brought back in by the current, though it is sometimes carried away to sea beyond where divers would be able to find it.

As surreal as this story is for him to read about in the morning paper, Fabian knows that if he has any trouble getting his car back today without the proper identification, the article should surely help prove who he really is. He tears the story from the newspaper and slides it into the smaller pocket of his red backpack.

Fabian looks over the bill when it arrives, remarks to himself that the quality of the food and service were well worth twelve dollars and reaches into the large section of his backpack for cash. Instead of a generous single twenty, which he would normally leave for a waitress as kind as this one, Fabian leaves for her the entire bundle of cash he has withdrawn from his bag. It's a stack of hundred-dollar bills, bound together at the bank with one of those thin rings of paper with the total value printed on it. Without looking to see how much the stack of cash adds up to, or even really caring about the amount, he sets the cash on the table, lays the check on top of it and covers it all with an unfolded napkin. Ellis would approve of this, Fabian is sure of it.

On his way toward the door, he smiles to the waitress, who is pouring fresh coffee into the cup of another patron.

"Do you need some change, sir?"

"No, you go ahead and keep the change. It's under the napkin there. And please try to make some time for your son."

"I'll certainly try," she returns. "You have yourself a nice day, sir."

As Fabian exits the diner and rounds the corner of the building, he passes by the booth where he had enjoyed his meal. The young waitress is there now, picking up the stack of money. She looks up through the window at Fabian with a bewildered stare. Fabian smiles, nods his head and keeps on walking down the sidewalk.

SIX

Making his way back toward the main road he turned off of after his less-than-friendly conversation with the beat cop earlier, Fabian is faced with the realization that all of his previous plans and backup plans have been made obsolete by the disappearance of his automobile.

No longer does he need to call a locksmith first, but the impound yard where his vehicle sits. No longer can he look forward to a greasy burger and fries handed to him from a drive-thru window, but to a salad or the soup of the day at a place where metal silverware is actually used. And no longer can Fabian count on driving home immediately, resituating himself and trying to get comfortable in his life that has become empty and not worthwhile lately.

He'll need to figure out a new plan, he knows, but a plan that is really no plan at all — just a roundabout solution to his current situation. Though not wanting to spend a second longer here than absolutely necessary, Fabian is also not looking forward to an empty apartment with dinner for one, a half-full washing machine taking care of an entire week's worth of laundry or receiving forwarded magazine renewal notices addressed to someone at his previous residence — the house with a white picket fence and a purpose. On top of all of this, Fabian is considered to be a dead man by the local authorities, a fate he wouldn't entirely mind at this point in his life.

A clear head is needed to figure this out, Fabian realizes, as well as complete physical relaxation — or as much of it as he can achieve here today. He's almost directly across the street from the park now, a place to which he really had no intention of returning. But with having no car in which to sit or a hotel room yet in which to lie down, Fabian knows a hard, dirty bench is his only realistic choice of seating.

He crosses the street at the first break in traffic — jaywalking, he knows, but that power-tripping police officer is nowhere in sight — and begins down a paved walking path into the depths of the expansive park, partially shaded in some areas from the burning sky by the partial-ceiling of decades-old foliage.

Finding one of the identical benches nestled under the thick overhang of branches of what

Fabian thinks is a large oak of some kind, he removes his shoes and socks, then rests his aching body as best as he can against the concrete slab, the top of his head at one edge of the seat and his knees bent so that his toes flirt with the edge at the opposite end. Like the night before, his lumpy red backpack is his pillow and he's clutching the garment bag tightly to his chest. He closes his eyes so that the blackness behind his eyelids become a blank board on which he can draw out his latest — and hopefully final — plan for getting himself home.

This plan will include many of the same elements of the previous ones, taking into account today's revelation that his car has been impounded and he may have actually drowned to death roughly thirty-six hours ago. To start, he will get directions to the nearest hotel from the first kind pedestrian he comes to, where he will shower and change into his clean suit. Still without any proper identification, Fabian may have to bribe the desk clerk if he's as much of a stickler to the rules as the last hotel employee he encountered. Once again looking presentable, he will call for a taxi from the phone in his room, and that cab shall take him to the nearest police station, where he will squash the rumors of yesterday's death, sort out the problems with his missing driver's license and be given directions to the impound yard holding his much-needed transportation home. From there, the plan resembles all the previous: drive straight home, stop at a fast food drive-thru if necessary, deal later with details like the broken car window, then sleep on through the weekend so that he's fresh and ready for work come Monday. Getting to San Francisco and taking care of his other business in this area will have to wait for another trip completely. This outing's been a bust.

Just as his plan comes together on the drawing board in his mind and he slowly starts to drift off to a peaceful slumber, the garment bag is ripped from his grasp and pulled away in a flash. Bolting up from the bench, Fabian looks around franticly, trying to figure out through his cloudy half-awake vision what has just happened. Far behind his bench, Fabian sees two men running toward the horizon, one of whom is carrying his garment bag and the other a guitar.

Scrambling, he slips on his socks but abandons his shoes as he knows he is losing precious time while the thieves make their escape with his only change of clean clothes. He sprints at full speed after them, the bottoms of his feet feeling every rock and broken twig hidden in the grass and his red backpack bouncing harshly between the back of his head and the small of his back. He knows the men — with shoes on their feet, a thirty-second head start and more knowledge of their surroundings than he has — have the clear advantage here. Fabian knows that he has no real chance at catching the men and that even if he did, he'd still be outnumbered two-to-one, but he'll be damned if he's going to lose any more of his personal property, especially to a pair of common street urchins.

Though far ahead of him, they are still well within his sight, and he plans to pursue them as far as his tired legs will allow him to. As they round another of the large, old trees, the man with the guitar is hit in the face by something unseen and falls backward to the ground with the guitar landing flat atop his chest. This startles both Fabian and the man's accomplice, who both stop running and instead stare in confusion and amazement at the man on the ground. The man with the garment bag is a few yards beyond the tree, wondering what his next move will be. Instead of assisting his fallen comrade, he turns away and proceeds to escape, Fabian now unconcerned with continuing the chase.

From behind the tree steps a man who appears to be as equally homeless as the robbers, shaking his hand in a manner that would suggest he might have broken it against the face of the man now sleeping at his feet. He's a black man wearing a dusty fedora, tall, lanky and obviously physically strong for a man in his late fifties. He looks at Fabian, then at the garment bag thief making his break. After kicking the other guy, still lying unconscious in the shade, squarely in the ribs, he bends over and retrieves the old guitar and walks cautiously towards the still-startled Fabian. As he gets closer, he hands the guitar off to Fabian, who takes it from the man without question.

"I wasn't fast enough to get that other guy, but we can catch up to him later," the guy tells Fabian. "This one here is Ricky, and I done talked to him before about stealing things from folks out here. It gives us all a bad name. But he don't ever listen to nobody. My name's Eddie Fred, by the way."

"This isn't my guitar," Fabian explains to Eddie Fred. "They had this already. All they got from me was that garment bag."

"A what bag? You know what? It doesn't matter," the talkative Mr. Fred continues. "You can either keep it or we can try to use it to barter for that bag you lost. That bag's his now; rules are rules."

"Nah, it's just a bag. If he needs it that bad, he can just keep it. I don't want to be here any longer than I need to be."

Fabian tries to hand the guitar back to Eddie, but the man doesn't accept it.

"You just hold onto that thing," the older man says. "I don't pick on no banjo, see. I blow the harp and sing the words. I need to have me a banjo picker for accompaniment, but I ain't got me a steady partner since back in last year sometime. Handsome Dave was his name, but he did some dude wrong and got himself shanked. It's a shame, too, 'cause we was good together, me and him, making some decent cabbage over here sometimes and over in Frisco, over by the piers and in Golden Gate Park. Had our own spot on a corner that nobody ever touched but us."

Eddie Fred pauses to give Fabian a good lookover.

"Boy, you ain't got no shoes on," he continues. "What your name?"

"Oh, I'm just passing through Santa Cruz, really," Fabian tells him. "I won't be staying here long. But thanks for your help."

"Nobody plans on staying here long, man," the guy persists, even after Fabian has started to walk away. "Everyone's just passing through here to someplace else — Frisco, Stockton, maybe Bakersfield. I'll be seeing you later on, banjoman. You find me and we'll go get your bag back."

Still carrying that stupid guitar, Fabian walks all the way back to his bench to retrieve his shoes. He doesn't care about that damned garment bag anymore. It's just one less thing for him to have to lug around until he gets his car back, though now he's holding onto an old guitar that he has absolutely no use for.

Back at the bench, his shoes are already gone. Even through the sand and the streaks, they were still nice-looking shoes and he knows it was a poor decision to leave them behind like that. He sits back down, then lies with the guitar across his belly and closes his eyes once again.

My car, my suit and now my shoes. All little things,

he knows, but losses just the same, though nothing compared to what is already gone from his life.

SEVEN

Depression is a dangerous disease not only for the individual personally inflicted, but by those who are in close contact with that person. It's highly contagious, spreading like a virus, with no known cure but medications that can sometimes suppress the symptoms for a while without actually making them go away, and that's only when the ill takes the pills as prescribed.

Tracy hated to take her pills. They were prescribed to her not long after Ellis was born, right around the time, as it were, that her only son — and the only child she would ever be able to create — was first diagnosed with acute lymphoblastic leukemia, brought on in part, Fabian is told, by his rough introduction into this world.

Some pills were antidepressants while others were to intended help her sleep at night. The antidepressants, the doctor warned, would likely cause insomnia, which could only make her depression worsen.

The child was weak but happy, more than could be said about Tracy. Fabian, on the other hand, always did his best to be strong for his family, and he carried the fate of his loved ones squarely on his shoulders — figuratively, of course, but foretelling, in a way, the inseparable bond he'd have with red backpack and its contents in the years to come.

Knowing the emotional strain his family's situation was taking on his wife, Fabian tried hard to be away from them as little as possible. But he still had a job to do back at the office, and the quality of his work performance was reflective of the turmoil he faced at home. While plugging away in his office, his thoughts were always on his wife and child at home.

Nothing, not even the treatments Ellis was already receiving, could help the little boy's physical health. Even through these stages of his sickness, the child never acted as though he was ill and he was very rarely ever without a smile on his face, partly due to his parents showering him with every toy imaginable. Fabian's job ensured the financial means were there to buy anything that brought the boy any sort of happiness.

Unfortunately, some things cannot be obtained with money, even with the best doctors money could buy. There was nothing anybody could do for Ellis beyond what was already happening, which was simply waiting to see if his body would react positively to the medicines and treatment.

Tracy's mental state was Fabian's main concern. Even when she took her pills, her rationale was skewed, and Tracy was prone to simply skipping scheduled doses of medication. She didn't need them, she often said, and only took them so Fabian would stop badgering her about it. If he wasn't home to make sure his wife was medicating herself, there was no telling what might be taking place there.

Fabian's fears were justified one day — Ellis must have been two years old at the time — when he returned home from work to what appeared to be an empty house. He first searched the living room, then the kitchen, and was making his way toward the stairs when he heard the faint cry of his son. In the family room at the rear of the house, Fabian could see his boy through the sliding glass doors leading to the back yard, only feet away from the family's swimming pool and wearing nothing but a diaper.

"It's okay, big guy, daddy's got you," the shaken father tried to reassure the toddler. "Where's mommy?"

Carrying the crying child, Fabian walked briefly to the pool, and then to the patio area before returning inside.

"Tracy?" He called out. "I'm home. Is everything alright?"

He knew, of course, that that everything was not alright. He briefly searched the remainder of the first floor, then climbed the stairs. The child's room was unoccupied, as were the bathrooms. Fabian's bedroom door was locked shut and all was silent inside. Fabian knocked on the door and called Tracy's name, but there was no answer. He carried Ellis back to the boy's room, gave him a toy to play with, then returned to the locked door.

"Tracy, baby, I need you to open the door," he pleaded with her. When that produced no results, he decided to bust through the door.

He took a step back, then lunged forward, planting his broad right shoulder into the middle of the door. It shook and rattled, but it did not open. He stepped back once more and kicked hard with the sole of his Italian leather shoe. This knocked the door open some, but something blocked it from moving further. Looking in, Fabian could see Tracy's leg. She was lying on the floor, still wearing the nightgown she rarely changed out of anymore. "Oh, God, Tracy!"

Pushing the door against the body of his wife, he squeezed his way into the room and snatched the cordless phone from its base on the nightstand, pressing the buttons as he jumped to the floor next to Tracy.

"Yes," he said franticly into the telephone. "My wife has just swallowed a lot of sleeping pills."

EIGHT

"You learn how to pick that banjo yet?" Eddie Fred is leaning over Fabian, tapping on the guitar body with his fingertips and arousing Fabian from an unintentional nap on that damned cement bench.

"See, I don't pick me no banjo. I just got me this here harp — or harmonica, if you prefer."

Sitting up, Fabian stares blankly at Eddie, hoping that the events during past few days were nothing more than a dream. Strangely, they seem more of a possible reality than what he left behind just a few days ago.

"Come on, man, it's getting dark out," Eddie tells him matter-of-factly. "It's warm now, but it's supposed to get colder later on. Heard somethin' about a cold front or somethin' like that."

"No, I'm alright," Fabian says. "Thank you, though."

"Come on, man," Eddie persists. "I ain't gonna hurt you, but your toes are liable to get frostbite there in them wet socks like that. Come on and I'll get you a pair of shoes to keep your toes from fallin' off."

Fabian thinks for a beat, then gets up. He's all alone and he hasn't even really thought seriously about where he's going to sleep tonight. He sure as hell doesn't want to traipse around town in socks. Besides, the man did give him a guitar, useless as it may be to him.

"What's your name, man?" Eddie asks, but to no response. "Where you comin' from to get yourself stranded here in Santa Cruz?"

Again, there is no response. Fabian's past is hard enough for even him to think about, and he doesn't need some complete stranger encouraging memories. Instead, Fabian just turns his head away from Eddie Fred as they continue walking down the park path, Fabian just a step behind the other man.

"Oh, I get it. You have some of that amnesia," Eddie says with a half-grin. "You're an amnesian. Lots of folks out here come with some amnesia. Sometimes it's the result of that post-traumatic stress, and sometimes the amnesia is voluntary. It doesn't really matter who you was, anyhow, wherever it is that you come from. Because everybody is someone else when they're out here on the streets."

Eddie abruptly steps sideways off the sidewalk,

and when Fabian doesn't follow, he reaches over and pulls his new friend off the path. Straight ahead is an oncoming jogger, who seems to not care who he might plow through on his run.

"Kick the branch, Tree Kicker!" Eddie shouts to the guy, who follows the command by jumping wildly into the air and karate-style kicking the tree limb overhead.

Upon a successful landing into a kneeling position, the Tree Kicker stands and resumes running.

"What you just witnessed was the mysterious Tree Kicker in action. They call him that because he kicks trees."

"Thanks. I picked up that much on my own. "

"That boy just runs around town, nonstop. Nobody knows when the man sleeps and nobody has ever seen the man eat. All he does is run around town like that, kicking a tree here and there if you request it. He's training for the 1984 Olympics."

"I think he missed it by a few years," Fabian jokes.

"Yeah, but he don't know that," Eddie explains. "You don't do any drugs, do ya?"

"No. Does everybody out here do drugs?"

"They do if they're dumb. You don't get yourself caught up in that stuff out here, ya hear me?

"Like I said, I'm just passing through. I'll be outta here by tomorrow."

"Yeah, like you said. Anyway, as close as anybody can figure, the Tree Kicker must've done himself a lot of drugs back in the day, most likely sometime before 1984. But he still has all those Olympic dreams floating around in his head and nobody out here dares to tell him what year today is. That guy just might kill you for squashing his dream like that, if you're able to talk to him in the first place. I heard the guy talk one time, and it wasn't in any language I've ever heard before. But he's harmless, anyway, just so long as you're not standing in front of him when he's running through."

"I'll keep that in mind."

"And I'll tell you another thing you gotta keep in mind, banjoman," Eddie lectures. "You gotta do yourself a favor and forget all them dreams you have right now in your head. Now, a man can't go around telling another man what to think — and honestly, a man can't rightly control his own damn thoughts — but you need to just keep them to yourself, and even out of your own mind if it's possible. Just turn the volume down on them, for your own sake. You just put those dreams on mute and you'll be fine. Just dream on mute."

By the time Eddie finishes his rant, the two men are steadily approaching a trio of homeless people conversing in the park.

"Who are they?" Fabian whispers.

"These folks are my friends, and they're your

friends, too. You'll need some friends out here," Eddie whispers back. "I'll get you some shoes, but only if you're friends, and friends have names. So, what's your name, man?"

"Hey, I'm not gonna be out here for very long."

"That's the plan, right?"

One of the men is younger, about Fabian's age, with a short, scruffy beard, shaggy brown hair, camouflage pants and a denim jacket with an American Flag patch sewn over the left breast pocket. Standing with him is the lone woman of the group and she appears to be his girlfriend. She is leaning against a cart — very similar to the luggage carts Fabian has used many times at various airports — that holds what seems to be both her and the man's belongings.

Beyond them stands a tall, older black man, heavyset with a graying beard and a faded maroon-colored knit cap. He speaks in a thick accent, possibly African, and he's staring at Fabian suspiciously.

"Eddie Fred, where the hell have you been?" the big man speaks loudly. "You get me what I sent you for?"

"Oh, yeah, Prince. It's right here." Eddie reaches into his pants pocket and retrieves something small and, keeping it concealed tightly in his palm, slides it into the other man's palm. This Prince doesn't look at it, just slides it immediately into his own pants pocket. Then he looks over to see Fabian watching the transaction.

"Eddie Fred, who is this man looking at me?"

"Who is this? Why, this here's Banjo Larry," Eddie tells him. "I'm teaching him how to pick on that banjo there."

"But you don't know how to play the guitar, Eddie," the young white homeless guy laughs.

"I know enough," Eddie fires back. "By the way, Jesse James, you're about his size. You got any extra kicks Banjo Larry can wear around? Someone stole my man's shoes from him."

"Well, that depends, man," Jesse answers, looking now at the man with the guitar. "You really gonna play some music with us?"

Without waiting for Fabian — or Banjo Larry, as Eddie has seen fit to rename him — to return an answer, Jesse turns to his girlfriend, who would be really attractive if she was to clean herself up a bit.

"Cricket, get them shoes out from the bottom there, from under my skins."

The young woman picks a bongo drum up out of the cart and digs under it for a pair of worn running shoes.

"Here," Jesse says to the man he knows only as Banjo Larry. "They still have most of the rubber on 'em. And if you need new strings for that guitar, I know where to get some."

"Does he need a jacket?" Cricket asks from behind.

"I don't know," Jesse tells her before turning

back to Banjo Larry. "Do you need a jacket? Yeah, you need a jacket. Cricket, he needs a jacket."

A large green military-style jacket is passed up from the cart and handed to the newest member of their little group, who doesn't want to take it but fears both the night's cold weather and possibly insulting the people after their show of generosity.

"Thanks," says the charity case, who probably has in his possession more money than ever seen by all the others there combined. "I'll get all of this back to you tomorrow."

"Nah, you keep that one. I got a few," Jesse tells him. "We need to lighten up the load, anyhow. We gotta be getting on up the road now, but we'll probably see you again tomorrow."

Jesse shakes his new friend's hand, then Eddie's, and begins pushing his cart down the sidewalk with Cricket at his side.

"Keep it real, Prince," Jesse says to the big man, who replies with a simple, "Uh-huh."

"Well, by your leave, Prince," it's Eddie's turn to bid the man farewell. "We gotta shove off, but we'll be seeing you around."

"Uh-huh."

Eddie Fred and the recently named Banjo Larry take the same path as the others, but in the opposite direction. Fabian doesn't really want to follow Eddie Fred, but he knows that he doesn't want to stay anywhere near the Prince.

"Why do you call him the Prince?"

"Because he's the Prince."

"The prince of what?"

"Take it from me, man, you don't wanna mess with that dude," Eddie insists. "I'll put it this way for you: I like you, man, but if the Prince comes to me tomorrow and says to kill Banjo Larry, I gotta kill Banjo Larry. That ain't gonna happen, though, 'cause I ain't no killer. I'm just being like hypothetical, but it's just a good idea not to piss that dude off."

Fabian decides not to push the issue. Chills run down his spine at the very thought that Eddie Fred might have to kill him at the whim of some guy who may or may not really believe he's some form of royalty.

"How'd you get out here, man?" Eddie changes the topic of conversation. "Was it that housing market crash? Yeah, I heard all about it. That's how Jesse and Cricket ended up out here. They've been out in this area for about a year now. Before that, they was in Frisco. I'm heading up there soon, for a little while, at least. You can come with me, if you're still out here, I mean. We can make some money playing out there by the piers. That's why you gotta learn you that banjo."

"Where are we going?" Banjo Larry interrupts his would-be mentor.

"We have to find us a place to crash for the night, somewhere to stretch our legs out up off the ground," Eddie tells him. "We're too far from my camp. On a Friday night, we'd have to walk past the clubs, and a man of the streets — like the two of us are — wouldn't do right to go interacting with the drunk college kids. You ever heard of Bum Burning?"

"Bum Burning?"

"No? Well, it's like an Olympic sport to these kids, if you get 'em drunk and ornery enough," Eddie explains. "That's extreme, mind you, but in the very least, they'll spit on you. And that just ain't something you'll ever get used to. Makes you wanna knock the sumbitch out, but that ain't ever a good idea. Who's the police gonna believe, a clean-cut college boy or some bum? As bad as it is out here, I'll still take my own camp over county lock-up any day of the week."

"Where is your camp?" He tries changing the subject again, to something less frightening.

"That's like an unwritten rule out here, man. You don't ask a man where he sleeps at night." Eddie is schooling his young protégé on hobo etiquette. "'Cause the next thing you know, you got fifteen dudes showing up the next night and your sleeping bag and cooking grill turn up missing."

As they approach a small grouping of young trees, Eddie points out a few benches nearby.

"Can you fight?" Eddie asks seriously.

"I'd really rather not."

"Yeah, but can you if you need to?"

"I don't know," Fabian responds, unsure

about the reasoning behind this line of questioning. "I used to box a little bit in high school."

"Alright then, you get that bench and I'll take this one. You gotta get 'em early before someone else does, or else you're sleeping on the grass. You watch my back and I'll watch yours. Tomorrow we'll start them banjo lesions."

With that, Eddie Fred stops talking and seemingly falls asleep quickly. Banjo Larry — he's tossing the name around in his head now — lies awake on his back, his red backpack still slung around his shoulders but pushed up under his head once again. The guitar is grasped tightly in both hands, pulled firmly to his chest. He considers waiting around for a little while, just long enough to know for sure that Eddie Fred is asleep before getting up to leave. *But then where would I go? And who might I run into?* At least Eddie Fred seems to have been honest with him. If the talkative old man was going to rob, hurt or kill him, he surely would have done it already when several opportunities must have presented themselves.

Soon Banjo Larry is also asleep.

NINE

Now, how does any man, homeless or otherwise, come to carry around a backpack full of money like that? That's a question that some people would literally kill to have the answer to. And if someone, perhaps this Banjo Larry, was to make it very well known in certain circles that he is such a man to possess a bag of money … well, that probably wouldn't turn out too well for the man with the bag.

But to answer that question, if it can be simply done, you might have to use a little bit of imagination or reasoning. You see, someone can win all that money, or they can steal it from someone else, or it can all be earned through ways legal or not.

For Banjo Larry, the money was earned, so to speak. A good amount of it was received in the form of paychecks from his big-budget employer.

Most of it, however, came from insurance payouts — his earnings, if you will, paid to compensate great loss.

The day Banjo Larry received that money — back before he was in fact Banjo Larry — he was a man of high standing and reputation within his community. Bankers called him Mr. Grunauer, not because it's polite customer service, but because it was men like him and the money they entrust to the banks that keep these places in business throughout the years.

It was on this day in particular that the bank manager herself was seeing to the needs of one of her most valued customers. But instead of depositing more currency into the vaults, he was withdrawing it all from his account, every last penny.

This bank manager — her name, it really doesn't matter — had a hard time understanding the man's reasons for making the withdrawal. Given the recent known events in this man's life, it was not unfathomable that he'd make some irrational, emotionally-based decisions. But really, she was just a bank manager, and it was none of her business to question the actions of men with Mr. Grunauer's status in society.

"That's all of it, sir," the bank manager said as she slid a plastic tote across her desk to him. "I'm sorry the process has taken so long, but we're not accustomed to turning over that large of an amount in cash. We'll have an armed security guard escort you out to your vehicle."

"Thank you, but that won't be necessary," he said as he stuffed the bundles of money into a crisp, new red backpack.

"But Mr. Grunauer," she insisted, "that's a lot of money right there."

"Exactly," he countered bluntly. "You think an armed guard walking me out to my car would be inconspicuous? And what happens after that? Will he escort me home, walk me to my front door?"

"I'm sorry, sir, I didn't mean to push. But I have to ask, why would you want it all in cash? That's a dangerous way to keep it. And not just for monetary reasons. I mean, the things some people would do to get a hold of all that cash."

"I know what you mean, ma'am, and I know what I'm doing."

"Oh, I trust that you do, sir. It's just that all this money represents your entire life savings, not to mention the proceeds from the sale of your house, and the life insurance." She paused, then gave him a pitiful look. "I read all about it in the papers, and I was so sorry to hear about it."

"I'm giving it all away," he interrupted her rambling.

"Giving it all away, you say? To charity?"

"Yes, that's right. I haven't figured out to which just yet, but probably to a children's charity of some type. That probably what Ellis would have preferred, I think."

"Well, that's a noble cause, Mr. Grunauer, for sure, but have you thought this decision through completely? I know your intentions are pure, but once you give it all away, that's it. You can't just unring a bell."

"Thank you for your concern, ma'am, but I have thought this through," he explained. "You see, without my family, I really don't have much use for the material things anymore — the big house, all that space, and the cars. I have found that fancy things just complicate life until you live for your possessions instead of just living for the sake of living. You really never fully appreciate what you have until you no longer have them."

After his backpack was stuffed full and zipped shut, he slung it over one shoulder and turned toward the door of her office.

"I don't mean to keep you hear any longer," she butted in again, "but you know that even charities accept checks. It really is much safer that way."

"Cash is safe enough," he insisted with a smile. "Besides, if you pay by check, there's no way to ensure that the donation remains anonymous."

TEN

Banjo Larry wakes up to Eddie Fred shoving a sandwich into his face.

"Get up, man, I made breakfast," the skinny black man urges his new friend. "We slept by the jungle gym. The fuzz don't like it when you're still sleeping here after the sun comes up. They say we scare the children. Eat your breakfast so we can get going."

Eddie slides onto the bench next to Larry and eats his own sandwich, then puts the jar of peanut butter and the half loaf of bread into his large canvas backpack. He removes two small red apples, hands one to his new partner as the young man finishes his sandwich. Eddie wasn't the sort of guy he'd normally trust to handle his food, but by now he's just plain hungry, having not eaten for about eighteen hours. He also doesn't want to insult the generosity of this potentially dangerous man, especially considering the guy is homeless and doesn't have much for himself, let alone any extras to spare for someone else.

"Come on," Eddie says, standing up and leading the way down the path. "You stay there, you're gonna get badgered by a cop. You best get a move on, boy."

Not wanting any trouble with any policemen, Banjo Larry follows closely behind Eddie and is soon right by his side on the sidewalk through the grass.

After a quick stop at the public restroom building in the park, the two men continue on out of the confines of the park and onto the cement walkways running parallel to the city streets. *What the hell,* Larry thinks to himself. *Maybe we'll pass a hotel somewhere and I can make a break for it.*

They come to an alley between a couple of small businesses and Eddie turns in and ducks between a couple of trash dumpsters.

"I just gotta look for something in here," he says.

"What are you looking for?" Larry asks in sincere confusion.

"Lunch," the older man says with a grin. "No, I'm just messin' with you, man. Here we go." He holds up a pair of plastic milk crates and carries them back out to the sidewalk.

The men, each lugging around one of the crates, stop near the corner diner Larry was in for breakfast just yesterday.

"I have to tell you, Larry, I don't really know how to pick on that banjo there," Eddie Fred admits. "But that shouldn't really matter. You just sit down on your box there and strum along the best you can. I'll blow on my harp and handle all the singin'. You just follow along, not too hard, and nobody will ever notice that you don't know what the hell you're doing there."

Before the duo starts into their first number, a skinny white woman in her late forties steps on up, holding a young black girl by the hand. She's pale and scary, and she standing toe-to-toe with Larry, just staring him in the eyes.

"You takin' requests today?" she asks, never taking hers eyes off of the man with the guitar.

"Not for you, Dorothy," Eddie snaps at her. "You don't know no songs, anyhow. You ain't never even heard no radio before."

"I got a radio, Eddie Fred, and I wasn't even talkin' to you. Who's your friend?"

"Here's a request for you, Dorothy," Eddie counters. "Get your nasty ass off my stage and take that thing there with you!"

Dorothy flips her middle finger up at Eddie and, dragging her child behind her in a huff, storms across the street and on down the road, her skinny ankles looking ready to snap in her comically-high heels.

"I don't know who that lady was," Banjo Larry scolds Eddie, "but you were pretty harsh on that kid, calling her a thing like that, right to her face."

"Oh, that thing's deaf, couldn't hear a damn thing I said," Eddie offers as an excuse. "You stay away from her, man. It ain't none of my business where a man seeks his pleasure, but that's one hooker you wanna stay away from." He pauses, giving Larry a concerning stare before continuing. "You knew she was a hooker, didn't you? You could've spotted that much, right?"

"Yeah, I think I could've spotted that much."

"Yeah, well she's one crazy ass bitch. That little boy of hers ain't got no chance, even if they had them a roof over their heads."

"Little boy?" Larry quips. "I think that little boy was a little girl."

"No, Banjo Larry, I know what I said. That little girl you saw was a male human person, just as you and me. That psycho got herself knocked up by Handsome Dave back before he got his ass shanked in the city."

"What city."

"Frisco, man, keep up," Eddie schools Larry. "Handsome Dave got stupid one night and paid her for a ride. Then he got some rash on his junk and he probably would've found some of that AIDS on him if he stuck around long enough. But, like I said, he got stupid and a certain somebody didn't like it and said Handsome Dave had to get gone."

"Was the Prince that certain somebody?"

"Damn, man, I talk too much, I know. But I ain't never said nothin' about that. You just forget what I said."

"So, what about that little boy in the dress?" Larry puts Eddie Fred back on topic before he has to sit through another rant.

"Yeah, well Dorothy the hooker didn't want a little boy. She wanted a baby daughter, so that boy's been wearing dresses and thinking he's a girl ever since he was born. That kid ain't never gonna be right."

"Did you shank Handsome Dave, Eddie?" *Why the hell would I ask him something like that?*

"Hell, Larry, I ain't no killer. Why would you even ask me something like that?" He stares at Larry coldly to drive the point in further. "Look at me, man, I'm a singer. Now sit down on that crate there and pluck that banjo."

Banjo Larry sits down, just as he's told, and Eddie Fred starts blowing on the harmonica he holds in one hand while slapping his leg with the other hand to keep time, doing a little bit of a stiff dance right there in place next to where Banjo Larry is sitting on the crate. Clumsily, Banjo Larry starts to strum on the guitar strings with his right thumb, doing something — he's not quite sure what — with his left hand to the strings at the end of the guitar's neck.

Eddie starts to sing a blues-sounding song, and his vocals are actually pretty good despite the lack of any actual music to accompany them. The song itself is sloppy and not very pleasant sounding at all, but it's better, Larry thinks, than one should expect given his nonexistent musical background.

This playing continues for several minutes, and a few songs into the set, Banjo Larry notices a woman drop some change into the fedora at Eddie's feet. All he sees of her is her legs — a little on the skinny side, but nice nonetheless in her skirt and sheer hose — and they stop right next to him, just short of the front entrance to the corner diner.

Now, Banjo Larry has seen a woman's legs before, and he's even been prone to gawk inconspicuously at the nicer ones, but these ones caught his attention even without there being anything really spectacular about them.

The legs back up ever so carefully and rest again directly in front of him. The woman's actions now, and not just her legs, have caught the full and undivided attention of the guitar player, who is now just holding onto the guitar motionlessly. His eyes follow the legs up, from her petite ankles to her knobby knees, and past them to her skirt, her blouse and nametag that reads Flo, then finally to her wide-eyed face. Banjo Larry is now staring into those eyes, the ones he noticed on the diner waitress over yesterday's breakfast.

Flo the waitress is staring at him as if she's caught looking into the face of her favorite celebrity.

"Is this where you work?" she asks him while

looking at his and Eddie's setup.

"Well, I guess so," he laughs. "This is my first day on the job, you could say."

"Hey, this is really awkward, but I wanted to thank you, you know, for the, uh, tip you left me. You have no idea what you did for us. I was hoping you'd come back around here. I really wanted to talk to you."

Eddie Fred stops playing his harmonica and stares over at Banjo Larry and the waitress.

"Do you live around here," she continues, "or are you ..."

"Larry, man," Eddie interrupts. "What's the deal here? We're losing business."

"Okay," she apologizes. "Well, are you gonna be out here for a while? I have to get in, anyway, but I can come out on my break. I really want to talk to you."

"Yeah, it looks like we'll be here, rain or shine."

"Untrue, Larry," Eddie butts in again. "If the rain hits, we're heading north two blocks. Stores have awnings there."

"Well, Larry," she smiles, "let's hope it doesn't rain then."

"Don't kid yourself, girl," Eddie Fred returns rudely. "Look up. It's coming. Come on, Larry, pick on that banjo and pluck the strings. It was nice meeting you, miss."

"Yeah, well if you aren't here, I'll know where to find you."

"Two blocks north," Eddie snaps at her before turning directly to his guitar player. "Now sit down on that crate and pick on that banjo."

Banjo Larry sits back down on the milk crate and puts the guitar back across his knees. The waitress opens the door and goes inside the diner. Larry starts to softly strum on the guitar as Eddie Fred begins to once again work up a melody of sorts on his harmonica. Soon, Eddie is singing the blues and Larry is thumbing along on the strings.

"Awe, hell," Eddie says before too long as he looks to the sky and jumps to his feet.

The waitress, now clocked-in and supposedly working, is staring out the window as raindrops fall on the pane of glass. Eddie Fred and Banjo Larry gather up their things and trudge down the road toward covered sidewalks. Larry looks back after a few steps to see Flo put her hand to the window. He gives her a quick smile and catches up quickly to Eddie.

"Like I said before," Eddie Fred tells Banjo Larry over his shoulder, "It ain't none of my business where a man seeks his pleasure, but that girl there sure was nice to look at."

ELEVEN

It's been said that the heart is mysterious, but it really isn't. It loves, it hates, it pumps blood, but really nothing more. The brain, on the other hand — well, there's just no point in trying to understand it sometimes.

You know, when Albert Einstein died, some New Jersey doctor removed the genius' brain from the body and saved it in a jar, just hoping to figure out what made the man so smart — even possibly smarter than his own good, as they sometimes say.

Would you believe that the reason Einstein had no intellectual rivals was because his brain was actually deformed? Yes, indeed, the man's brain was larger than the average, by comparison, and certain grooves that were supposed to run through it were not as defined as they should have been — or nonexistent, in some instances.

These grooves would separate two sections of a normal brain, where information is transferred back and forth. Well, with the absence of the deep grooves, the sides of Einstein's brain were closer together and the information could travel between them much easier and much quicker. If it were not for his retarded brain, Einstein would have been no genius at all.

Tracy, as it seems, had herself a retarded brain. She was no genius like Einstein, nor was she a child in the body of an adult, as it usually might turn out for folks. Instead, she had problems with her emotions and with keeping those emotions from causing herself and those around her some serious harm. The problem was largely unnoticed throughout her childhood and early adulthood, but after the difficult birth of Ellis, her condition appeared as a mental sickness that had no cure but only medicinal treatments.

After her son was diagnosed with his own life-threatening disease, Tracy's mental health had deteriorated to the point that her husband was forced to hire a nanny to help tend to their child while the father was away at work. Tracy resented the fact that her significant other didn't trust her enough with her own child, and resented the nanny because of the perception that this other woman was moving in on her territory and might ultimately serve as her replacement.

The nanny, an attractive middle-aged Hispanic woman named Diana, knew the circumstances which resulted in her being hired by the family. Diana knew that Tracy was not well, that she drank more and more each week and that the wife and mother was prone to irrational outbursts when her place in the family felt threatened. The nanny had on a few occasions called her employer while the man was at the office, complaining of the abuse at the hands of his wife. It was only after pleading, promising and the occasional monetary bonus that he was able to keep her in his employment.

One day, however, Diana had simply had enough. She called to tell him that she could no longer handle working there and that he needed to come home immediately.

The nanny was sitting on the sofa when her employer opened the front door, but stood up as soon as he walked in, already wearing her sweater and holding her purse. From her black eye, scattered hair and red face, it was quite clear that some type of violence had occurred there just moments before.

"She hit me this time and I cannot take this any longer from her," Diana said. "I would've left already but I didn't know what she might do to that boy."

"She was hurting him!" Tracy screeched from upstairs as Ellis cried wildly from her arms. "I won't have that woman hurting one hair on his head! You hear me?"

"Sir, I was just changing his diaper, same as I

always do, and she attacked me," the nanny explained. "I like you, sir, I really do. And I love that little boy, but I'm leaving here now and I won't be coming back in the morning."

"Diana, I completely understand, and I'm sorry." He handed her several twenty-dollar bills, folded in half. "Here, take this, and again, I'm so sorry."

"Thank you, sir," she said. "I really hope she gets some help, for the sake of Ellis. I really think she could hurt that boy."

"You're always taking her side!" Tracy cried from the top of the stairs as the door shut behind the nanny. "You stay away from me! I can't trust you anymore!"

As he climbed the stairs, he could see that she held their two-year-old son in her arms and she was dangerously close to the banister, high above the family room.

"What are you going to do when he's gone?" Tracy plopped Ellis onto the floor between her feet and stormed into her bedroom. "I can't make you any more! What are we going to do when he's gone?"

TWELVE

Banjo Larry sits alone now, and that's just fine by him. While he's somewhat thankful for the usual company of the talkative Eddie Fred lately, he does enjoy his personal time that he can quietly reflect on his past and take wild guesses at his future.

What's the deal with Eddie, anyway? Larry asks himself. *What's his angle? What is it that he wants from me? It can't really be my guitar playing?*

He hasn't seen the old man in a couple of days, and while he doesn't miss Eddie specifically, he does sometimes miss having someone to talk to, and Eddie Fred could certainly carry on a conversation, with or without Banjo Larry's assistance. On some nights, when Eddie doesn't feel like making his way back to his own camp, he'll sleep in this area of the park near the new guitar player, telling him all about his past but never asking Larry to reveal any more details of his, as he knows Banjo Larry has not yet gotten any past to speak of.

"Just find you a corner and make some lunch money," Eddie would tell his buddy before leaving on these trips, probably running some errand for the Prince. "Sing some songs or just sit there looking pathetic. Either way, someone's bound to toss you a few pennies eventually."

And Larry would play his guitar for the people, but it wasn't for the money. Maybe it was out of boredom, or his willingness to try new things and learn a new trade. Either way, Larry would take these breaks from Eddie Fred as opportunities to eat well by paying for his meals from the cash in his red backpack. Sometimes it was fast food, sometimes it was something from a grocery store, and sometimes he filled up at a nice sit-down diner, like the one where he met that nice young waitress.

He hasn't seen her there, though, not since that day several weeks ago when he ran into her there in front. She must've quit, he figures, taking his advice to spend more time with her son. He hopes so, but he also hopes she doesn't just blow through that free cash buying useless junk until she finds herself once again broke and unemployed. Larry imagines her crawling back to the diner and asking for her old miserable job back, finding herself back in the same situation he tried to help her out of.

That's the problem with folks these days, always looking for a handout but never willing to work to get ahead, he says to himself, before grinning. *And all this coming from a shiftless bum.*

Without Eddie's harmonica and singing, Larry would starve to death if he relied on his own earnings now to eat. Though he's not really taking his playing very seriously, he made just enough between this morning and all day yesterday to make a few calls from a payphone.

He could call his old boss and see if he still has a position at the company. He could call the police and tell them he never drowned, or the impound yard to ask them about getting his car back. Or he could call himself, so to speak, and see what others have been saying to him when he wasn't listening.

Down the street, about halfway through the park along the sidewalk, is a pair of payphones standing back-to-back. He digs through his heavy pocket and counts out exact change, then drops it into the slot.

He dials his old phone number. After several rings, the robotic female voice of the answering machine begins to speak. *You have reached the voice mailbox of area code two zero nine, eight three ...* Larry presses the pound button. *Please enter your security code.* Larry presses the five buttons that make up his code and waits. *You have thirty-seven new messages. Press one to hear your messages.*

"Mr. Grunauer, this is Sandy," started the first

message, from one of the secretaries at his old job. "Mr. Reynolds was just wondering if you were going to be out for the rest of the week or if you were coming back in tomorrow. Either way is fine, but he just wanted to know what your plans were so we could shift some meetings around or have Mr. Dent just cover the meetings for you if you wanted to take some extra time off. Please give someone here a call and let us know what's going on, the sooner the better. Thank you."

Delete. Next.

"Yes, this is Sergeant Davis with the Santa Cruz Police Department. I'm trying to reach somebody from the Grunauer household. This is an important matter and we need to speak with someone there, please. I'll be contacting someone from the police department there in your town, so maybe they'll be able to talk to you easier than I can. But if you get this message soon, please call me back at …"

Delete. Next.

"Hello, this is Detective Mike Sandoval and I'm following up on a call I got from the police department out in Santa Cruz. They're looking for a Fabian or Tracy Grunauer regarding a vehicle that they towed out there. Also, there was a report of witnesses out there seeing someone possibly abandon the car, from what I gather, and they're looking for that individual, possibly Mr. Grunauer, who may or may not have left the scene, well, through the water. I don't usually leave messages like this, but I came by the house listed in your vehicle registration information and you no longer live there. I found a possible address for you at an apartment on Granite Boulevard, but there was no answer there when I knocked. If this is the correct phone number, if this is the Grunauer residence, if someone there could please call me back, that would be really helpful. I'll stop by that apartment again later today to see if someone's home at that time, but if you get this message ..."

Delete.

Larry hangs up the phone. Whoever they've all been looking for is dead now. That whole Grunauer family is dead. The last member of that little clan drowned out here in Santa Cruz some weeks back.

THIRTEEN

As far back as he can remember, he hasn't lost too many people who were close to him in life. Sure, he's had friends, like everybody else, who've moved away over the years. He also vaguely remembers some grandparents who passed away when he was very young, and knew that his other grandparents were dead before he was even born. Those lost friendships and old-age deaths never really affected him at all, one way or another. Then, all at once, sadness surrounded him, and the two people he loved the most were gone from his life.

Ellis, his son from the previous life, was the first to go, but not like you may have expected. Yes, he was a sickly child, and his illness did, in a way, ultimately lead to the boy's death, but not directly.

And once Ellis was dead, Tracy apparently felt

that she could no longer live happily with her husband and she left him also, though not in the same way and with much more say in the matter than what Ellis had.

Sometimes, the treatment one receives for their ailment is actually a poison, intentionally administered by trained and knowledgeable medical professionals to attack and eradicate the disease from the body. And that poison, while doing its part to kill the evil, will usually take a toll on the good. The goal of this type of treatment is to kill the infestation of sick cells so that the healthy ones have a fighting chance at taking over. And that was the case with the treatment of young Ellis, though not with the success hoped for.

"Mr. and Mrs. Grunauer," the doctor said while they were seated in his office. "The chemotherapy doesn't seem to have worked."

"So that's it?" Tracy was in shock. "How could it not work? Look at him, for God's sake. The chemo's just about killed him, and the cancer's still there?"

The boy, just past four years old and sitting fragilely in his father's lap, was thin and bald, his pale eyes staring blankly from deep pockets in his boney skull.

"The chemotherapy doesn't always work," the doctor explained. "And sometimes we can go in for another round once he's strong enough to handle it, but not right now. If we continue with the chemo, he won't survive it."

"So then that's it? We just give up?"

"No, we wait to see how he does and we'll possibly try more later on when we feel he can handle it. But for now, we're looking at maybe some radiation therapy and we need to look for a match for a bone marrow transplant. We're not completely out of options here."

"You're not gonna let my baby die," Tracy scolded the man behind the desk. "You're gonna do whatever you possibly can to make sure my son lives. Do you hear me? Whatever the cost, I don't care if we have to fly to some other country with better doctors or if we have to fly those doctors here to replace you people, but my son is not gonna die. Do you hear me?"

"Yes, ma'am, I hear you," the doctor answered calmly and politely. "And I assure you, everything that can be done for Ellis can be done right here, and our doctors are more than qualified to do it. These things take time, and things sometimes get worse before they get better. Whatever we can do to save your son's life will be done, I promise you that."

FOURTEEN

Banjo Larry and Eddie Fred are in the center of the park, along with Jesse and Cricket, where two of the major sidewalks through the park intersect. Each of them is supplying their parts to the makeshift street band and the music they play sounds almost good enough to stop and listen to, which some folks around there do, for a little while.

While Eddie sings and plays his harmonica, Jesse slaps rhythmically on his bongos and Cricket sings the harmony vocals softly and sweetly. Larry, still in his learning stages, strums his guitar the best he can. He's still not any good with it — not by a long shot — but at least he's more comfortable with the instrument, having by now a couple of months' worth of practice.

When that song — an old blues number that nobody except Eddie really recognizes fully — is over, Cricket starts into a folksy tune and everyone else joins in. Larry, never having been much of a music scholar, doesn't recognize this one, either. Jesse might, as he's playing right along with it. But then again, Jesse seems to be able to keep time with any song they're struggling through. He's thankful for any chance he can get to play music with others, as his drumming just sounds out of place when accompanying only Cricket's voice alone, which is somewhat reminiscent of Maria Muldaur in her youth.

The Tree Kicker runs toward the group and Eddie takes a break from his playing to give the traditional instructions to the crazy man.

"Kick the tree, Tree Kicker," Eddie yells while pointing to a branch shading the band. "You kick that tree, Tree Kicker."

As per usual, the Tree Kicker goes through his routine of kicking upward at the limb and kneeling upon a graceful landing before resuming his run.

"Good, Tree Kicker, now run away from here," Eddie encourages as he goes back to blowing on his harp. As people casually walk past them, Eddie breaks into dance — sort of a shuffle, actually — and points down to the fedora lying at his feet with the hand not holding the harmonica to his lips. One man, walking arm-in-arm with a lovely woman, digs into his pocket and tosses a handful of loose change into the hat. Eddie shows his appreciation by stepping up his dance while the couple passes, leaving the group with absolutely no audience for at least a hundred yards in any direction.

"I need to save my voice for the lunchtime crowd," Eddie declares as soon as Cricket's song is completed. "It's your turn there, Larry. Sing a song for our fans."

"I don't think so," Larry smiles.

"I don't think so?" Eddie repeats. "You can't just sit there plucking on them banjo strings. You gotta pull you own weight around here."

"I can't sing," Larry returns. "I can't even play the guitar properly."

"I'll sing again," Cricket offers. "Let's play *Gallows Pole.*"

"No, honey, we need to save your voice for when people are actually listening," Eddie says to her. "It's Larry's turn to sing a bit. So come on, boy. Ain't nobody around to hear you but us. Give it a try."

"What about him?" Larry tries desperately, pointing to a guy on a bike with a huge industrial-sized plastic trash bag hanging from each end of his handlebars. The man is leaning over his bike and digging through a trash can for recyclables, paying absolutely no attention to the two men bickering about taking turns.

"Who, Willie Nelson's Dead?" Eddie turns to the guy, a man with close-set semi-crossed eyes, a 1980s-style puffy jacket and odd-fitting tight jeans. "Hey, Willie Nelson's Dead!"

"Shut up!" returns the angry simpleton, an obvious fan of the Red-Headed Stranger who no doubt earned his street moniker from the taunts people throw at him constantly. Antagonizing this guy is another local ritual started way back when and continued on throughout the years by folks who get their jollies from seeing the man fume.

"No, you shut up!" Eddie counters.

Willie Nelson's Dead jumps off his bike and walks angrily toward the band — huffing, puffing and unzipping his fluffy jacket.

"Oh, no you don't," Jesse mutters as he jumps up from his bongo drums. He meets Willie Nelson's Dead on the sidewalk and stares him in the eyes. "Willie Nelson's Dead."

"Shut up!"

Jesse raises a clenched fist and steps forward very threateningly. Without so much as a swing from Jesse, the man known as Willie Nelson's Dead flinches and ducks backward.

"Get the hell outta here!" Jesse warns as he lowers his hand.

While Jesse returns to his drums, Willie Nelson's Dead zips up his silly puffy jacket, picks up his bike and rides away with the trash bags dangling from the handlebars, each almost dragging the ground and doing their part to help gravity knock the simple man to the pavement.

"You may continue, Banjo Larry," Jesse says politely as he sits on his milk crate.

Without argument, Larry begins to strum the

guitar strings lightly but mechanically. *Swing low, sweet chariot* ... Immediately, Eddie Fred begins to blow along on his harmonica, Jesse taps his drum lightly while Cricket sings soft harmony vocals.

As the group plays and Larry sings, several folks walk by and some even throw their change into Eddie's fedora. A few people actually stop and listen to the song until it's over, then toss in some change and a few dollar bills and walk away.

"You're on a roll, banjoman," Eddie encourages him. "Do another."

"But I don't know any other songs."

"Come on, Larry, keep the momentum," Jesse joins in.

Reluctantly, Larry begins, but to more embarrassment than with the last song. *Some days I hate you, some days I love you, some days it's one and the same* ...

Eddie Fred tries to pick up the melody and plays along, as does Jesse. Once Cricket realizes the reoccurring lines that would serve as the chorus, she sings those parts with Larry, humming softly with the rest of the song. After the third verse, a string on the guitar snaps and causes everyone to stop.

"Just play through it, man," Eddie tells him.

Larry starts to strum again while the others resume their parts, but the sound is worse than usual.

"Okay, man, just stop," Eddie scowls. "You need a new string. Take a break from that before you drive away our fans."

By now, Larry is relieved to see that there is absolutely nobody on the sidewalk within hearing range.

Jesse asks, "What song was that, man? I didn't recognize it."

"Nothing. Just something I had in my head."

"Oh, so you're a songwriter now, eh?" Eddie criticizes. "Next time, write something with a groove. Jesse's just sitting over there gathering dust on that last one."

Eddie picks up his fedora and sorts through the money in it. He scoops out the bills, pours the change into his palm and hands the coins to Larry.

"Now go two blocks up that way and three more to the right and buy you a new string for that banjo," he orders the young man. "There's a store up there selling banjo strings."

"No, come on, Eddie. That money's for all of us," Jesse complains. "And he can't even play that guitar."

"Then we'll have no problem making that little bit of money back while he's gone then. Now start slapping them skins and get us an audience."

Larry shoves the money into his pocket and begins walking down the cement path toward the street as the rest of the band begins to play and Cricket starts singing Bob Dylan's *Blowin' In The Wind*.

FIFTEEN

Just a pocket full of change. That's all his life is worth now.

On one hand, a pocket full of change is an awfully small amount to show for himself, especially after the kind of money he used to rake in, or the kind of money he has secretly stashed in his red backpack. On the other hand, however, Larry now realizes that he doesn't really need any more than a pocket full of change to get by. That little peace of mind alone is sometimes worth giving up the luxury of a padded bank account.

Aside from the annoyances of the never-ending jingling sound and having his pants weighted down while the bulk of the coinage constantly beats against his thigh as he shuffles down the road, funding his life with spare change discarded by others isn't as difficult as he had previously believed it might be.

But then again, Banjo Larry is a special case amongst the street urchins. He does, after all, have a seemingly endless emergency relief fund just within arm's reach.

Not really being a guitar player, Larry wonders if the coins would even pay for a guitar string. It doesn't really matter since he'll most likely pay with the paper money strapped to his back. He needs to keep the change for later, he knows, as keeping up appearances is important to him. He knows that, with his relatively limited experience with living on the streets, he's a far cry from having the abilities folks like Eddie Fred possess in regards to monetary intake. He can pull in enough each day for maybe one of his meals, but at that rate he'd shrivel up to skin and bones in no time. And it's not as if he could simply whip out a hundred-dollar bill whenever he's short on lunch money. So he spends the money from the backpack wisely and saves the coins for when he knows Eddie is watching.

Coming to a payphone, Larry decides to check some old messages pertaining to some other life in some alternate universe. He drops the correct change into the slot and dials his old phone number, and a familiar female voice speaks, though not the voice he had expected to hear.

"Hello?" she says. "Hello?"

Why the hell was she in my apartment? Who the hell gave her a key?

"Is there someone there?" the voice continues.

"This is Gayle Grunauer, Fabian's mother. If someone is there, could you please answer me?"

Banjo Larry slams the phone down and walks away quickly.

"That's the last time I dial that number," he mutters aloud.

SIXTEEN

Larry stands in front of the music store two blocks up and three blocks to the right from the area of the park in which he left Eddie, Jesse and Cricket making music — and hopefully some money — without him. He plans to enter the store to buy his replacement guitar string, but for now he is simply gazing through the plate glass window at the storefront where some featured instruments are displayed.

How much is that guitar in the window, the black one with dials and chrome, Larry smiles to himself as he leans into the window to inspect the guitar's price tag. *Sweet Jesus, who in their right mind would pay that much for a guitar?*

Larry takes a step back to get a better look at the whole display, which also includes a couple of bass guitars and an electric keyboard. Most of the guitars are stylish electric models that Larry knows he will never be able to play, even if he wanted to be a damned guitarist in the first place. Between the necks of the guitars, he spots a man staring at him from behind the counter on the opposite side of the store. Larry walks into the building and goes directly to that counter.

"Can I help you, sir?" the salesman asks politely. "Maybe you'd like to get out from that worn-out flat top box and upgrade to a newer model?"

"No, thank you. I just need to purchase a new string to replace this one that broke," Larry tells him.

"You wanna buy one string to replace the one that broke? And exactly which string is it that broke?"

"It's one of the middle strings," Larry explains, holding up the guitar for the man to see. "The rest are fine. I just need to replace that broken one."

"Yeah, well, we only sell guitar strings in sets, so you'll have to buy all six if you want that one. You can either keep the other five as replacements for when they eventually break, or you can just replace them all right now. But some of those others there are rusty, and they're all stretched out. How old are these strings?"

"They were on the guitar when I got it, so I don't know."

"How long have you had the guitar?"

"I don't know. Maybe three months."

"Yeah? How long have you been a guitar player?"

"Since the day I got the guitar."

"I see," the man smiles. "I suppose you're gonna want me to tune it for you?"

"With the way I play, I don't think tuning it really matters much."

"I'll go ahead and tune it for you, anyway," the salesman laughs. "Free of charge. Give me about an hour and I'll have it all ready for you. Feel free to look around the store. Maybe you'll change your mind about upgrading."

"No, I'll be back in about an hour. Thank you."

As Larry makes his way back outside, he's met by Flo, the waitress from the diner. Though she doesn't say anything to him at first, he's caught off guard and he stops and stares at her.

"Hey, I saw you walking and I saw you go inside there," she says sheepishly. "I was just waiting out here for you to come out. I hope that's not weird."

"No, I'm just getting my guitar fixed. Are you on your way to work?"

"No, I just got off. You wanna walk with me, maybe get something to eat? My treat."

"Your treat? Well, I haven't really had lunch yet."

Larry and the waitress walk down the city sidewalk, not saying a word, until they come to a small American food restaurant with outside seating.

"Burgers okay?" she asks him.

"I'd love a burger," Larry replies.

Flo tells the man behind the counter, "Two burgers, two fries and two Cokes, please."

The couple is sitting at a small table when the food is brought out to them.

"So, your name's Larry?" the young woman starts the conversation.

"Uh, yeah, I guess so. That's what they call me out here, at least. And I see that your name is Flo."

Flo laughs. "No, not really. It's more of an inside joke and a safety precaution rolled into one."

Larry gives a confused look, and so she explains. "Around here, some diner patrons tend to get attached to the waitresses. So when I first started working at the diner, some of the other girls advised me to pick an alias."

"So that's the safety precaution. Where's the inside joke?"

"You probably don't watch too much television. Am I right? And not too many movies?"

"No, not lately."

"Well, it seems like every diner waitress in every movie and every TV show is named Flo. When the girls asked me what I wanted my fake name to be, that's all I could think of. So at work, my name is Flo, but everywhere else, my name is

Virginia."

"Virginia," Larry repeats. "It's a pretty name."

"You know, I never used to think that before people started calling me Flo all the time," she smiles innocently.

"Aren't you worried about me becoming attached to you now that I know your real name?"

"No, actually, I'm worried that you should think I've become attached to you," she explains. "You see, Larry, it's true that seeing you from down the street today was pure coincidence, being at the right place at the right time, but I have been watching for you."

"Yeah, why's that?" Larry asks while taking another bite of his burger.

"Because I missed you that last time. I went down to where you said you were gonna be playing, but it was storming pretty hard. I figured you guys went home early. But I still wanted to talk to you."

"Talk to me about what?"

"Oh, come on. Talk about what? What do you think I want to talk about?"

Larry shrugs, looks the other way and tosses a few fries into his mouth.

"That was a lot of money, Larry. I mean that was more money than I've ever seen before, let alone all at once and in cash. Where did it come from?"

"From my backpack, Virginia. It's mine. It's

not stolen. It's mine."

"Is there more?"

"Why? Do you need more?"

"No, I don't need any more! That was more than enough that you gave me."

"You didn't invest it, did you? It's better to spend it now while you're able to."

"Well, you can say I spent a bunch of it as an investment." Larry gets a puzzled expression on his face, so Virginia continues. "I got caught up on my rent. They were gonna evict me because I was so behind, and now I'm ahead. And I enrolled in school full-time, Larry. I'm gonna be a nurse."

"Full-time, and you're still working at the diner?"

"I'm only at the diner part-time now. I quit my other job, though. I like having at least a little bit of income coming in, so I just took reduced hours at the diner. Where did the money come from, Larry, and why did you give it to me?"

"You seemed nice and you had a picture of your kid and you looked like you could use a little bit of help, that's all."

Virginia just stares at Larry with her mouth gapped open slightly, as if she is searching for the right words to say. "Nobody gives out that kind of money just being nice."

"Look, can we just move on past the money?"

"Fine, then," she agrees. "Where do you live, Larry?"

"I have a place nearby."

"Does it have a roof, Larry? Are there walls on this place of yours?"

"Hey, I thought you wanted to talk, but you're just here yelling at me. What are you accusing me of?"

"Nothing! Nothing," she takes a deep breath. "What are you hiding from? You live on the street with a backpack full of money ..." She stops talking mid-sentence, looks around for anybody who may have heard her, and then continues in a quieter voice. "You give a waitress who smiles at you a stack of cash while your clothes look like they haven't been cleaned in years. Are you in trouble with the law?"

"No, I've never even gotten a speeding ticket."

"So you have a car? Is that where you sleep?"

"No, I used to have a car. And I used to have a wife and son."

"But not anymore?"

"No, not anymore."

"Do they know you're out here? How do you know they're not wondering where you are. How do you know your son isn't missing you right now?"

"Because he's dead, that's why."

"I'm sorry," she looks down, embarrassed. "I didn't mean to pry. I'm sorry."

"Yeah, well, back there, everyone knew us and now all *they* do is pry. But out here, nobody asks me about my son or anything else from back then. I didn't mean to end up out here, but it's honestly easier than going back there with everyone's pity and their concern." Larry laughs a little. "You know, I bet there's probably more folks than I realized back there wondering where I've been."

"And what town was that, the town where you're from?"

"You know, I still have a house there, well an apartment now, actually. I did have a house, a big house, but I couldn't live there afterwards. I sold it and got a tiny one-room apartment. I bet that apartment manager is wondering where the rent money is."

"How did your son die, Larry?" As soon as she asks, the man's eyes well up with tears. "I won't ask you about your family anymore, Larry. I'm sorry."

"I have to go," Larry says. "My guitar is probably ready now. Thank you for lunch." He stands up from his seat and puts on his red backpack.

"Larry, I'd like to see you again. Can you come by the diner sometime?" But the man does not seem to hear her and continues to walk away without responding. "Larry?"

SEVENTEEN

Banjo Larry, a shy person by nature, does like to expand his circle of friends and meet new people. Police officers, specifically, as much as he may respect the work they do, are never individuals Larry has ever wanted to meet.

Nowadays, they get after him for vagrancy, loitering, jaywalking, panhandling and just being a public nuisance in general. These occurrences are really nothing more than a verbal lashing by a bored cop just out flexing his muscles of authority. Back in the old days, however, the occasional visit from a cop proved to be a bit more serious.

There were a few times when the neighbors called the police to report a domestic disturbance after one of Tracy's screaming tirades. The husband is always initially suspected by police to be the cause of all domestic problems, but after it was explained that Tracy had skipped a dosage of her medication, the cops would complete the notes for their reports and leave without too much incident. After a few of these calls, the responding officers knew what to expect and they would start off by asking if Tracy had been taking her pills or not.

Then there was the call that was made not by a concerned neighbor but from inside their own house.

"My wife has just swallowed a lot of sleeping pills." The plea for help still echoes through Banjo Larry's cranium whenever he's so unfortunate enough to think about that night.

But the night that really haunts the man is the one when Tracy herself called the police out to the house. Her husband was not home at the time, having just left but a few minutes prior to the call being placed. He would've dialed the number himself, but he was too distraught and felt the need for nicotine, a habit he had given up without struggle several years earlier. He simply and ever so quietly walked out his front door and slid into the front seat of his car, then drove it down to the nearest convenience store and purchased a pack of cigarettes and a disposable lighter. He smoked one in the parking lot while standing nervously next to his car, and then he smoked another one.

Not long afterward, maybe an hour or slightly more after leaving his driveway last, he steered his car back toward home. From a couple of blocks away, he could see the lights flashing, illuminating the entire night sky like the Fourth of July. The neighbors were all outside, up far past their bed times, witnessing the most exciting event in the modern neighborhood's short history. There were a few squad cars and an ambulance, and the paramedics at the scene appeared to be in no hurry at all.

He knew that he'd have to deal with the authorities at some point during the night, but having them meet him at the curb in front of his house was completely unexpected.

"Mr. Grunauer?" the first cop met him as soon as he stepped foot on the lawn. "Is this your home, sir? Is your wife Tracy?"

"Yes, sir," he responded solemnly, still walking toward the front door of the house.

"Sir, you can't go in there," the officer stopped him with a hand on the shoulder as another policeman walked past, to whom the first cop whispered in the ear, "Has the chaplain arrived yet?"

"Where's my wife?"

"Mr. Grunauer, we know that your wife was supposed to be taking some antidepressants," the cop continued. "And I know that we've come out here before for some domestic issues when she hadn't taken them."

"Yes," the husband responded. "Where is she? Did she tell you what happened?"

"Sir, where were you just now?"

"Just now? I was buying cigarettes, but I was here at home before that."

"And how long would you say you were gone?"

"I don't know," he answered. "An hour, maybe an hour and a half. I needed to clear my head."

"Were you home when your wife called us?" the cop continued.

"No, I didn't know she called you. Where is she? Where's Tracy?"

"Sir, was there an argument here earlier between you and your wife, before you left?

"No, there wasn't any argument. My son was sick. I just needed to go clear my head. What did she tell you happened?"

"Your son's dead, Mr. Grunauer," the policeman stated bluntly. "Your wife smothered him with a pillow before she called us."

"No, she didn't," he insisted. "Is that what she told you?"

"She called 911 and said 'My baby is dead' and put the phone down. The 911 dispatcher could still hear her moving around for a while, but your wife wouldn't answer back when the dispatcher tried talking to her. When officers arrived, there was no answer at the front door but it was unlocked. Because of the call your wife had made from inside the house, the officers thought it necessary to enter the premises, where they found your son deceased in his bed and your wife deceased in the bathroom."

"Deceased? What the hell are you talking about?"

"Sir, it looks like your wife swallowed an entire bottle of sleeping pills. We found the empty bottle lying next to her body, along with the pillow from your son's bed. Considering the history of calls we've received here and given your wife's history of depression, we think she used the pillow to smother your son to death before taking her own life."

"No, that's not what happened."

"I understand that this is difficult, sir, and we have a chaplain on the way down here if you need to talk to someone," the cop tried his best to console the man. "Sir, we're gonna be here for a while as part of the investigation. Is there someplace else that you can go tonight, maybe you have family nearby or one of your neighbors? We'll need to talk to you more tomorrow, but it's probably not a good idea that you be alone tonight."

"No, there isn't anybody. My whole family is there in that house."

EIGHTEEN

Banjo Larry hesitantly allows his eyes to open, the dim artificial lights hanging high above making it impossible for him to continue sleeping while he wishes he could get just a few more minutes of quality rest. And he could really use the sleep today, his face bruised with a black eye and a cut on his bottom lip, all results of the events that took place a few nights ago. Now, that was a hell of an evening.

But this morning, Larry finds himself on a small cot, surrounded by what appears to be hundreds of identical cots, each one supporting the weight of one homeless man with his belongings stuffed below it — all except for the cot right next to his own.

"Where's Eddie?" Larry calls out quietly. "Hey, Jesse, where's Eddie?"

"Go back to sleep, man. Jesus Christ, what's

wrong with you?" Jesse is curled up on his own cot nearby, wrapped up tightly in his blanket.

"Where's Eddie?"

"Shut up, man." Jesse sits up, squints into the overhead lights and then stares at Larry. "You know why I come here each winter instead of staying outside? It's not because I can't handle the cold. Believe me, I can handle that cold. It's because it's not coed. The women have to sleep in a room in the building next door. It cuts down on the fornicating. But for me, that means that for one season each year, I don't have to wake up to some whiney voice at the crack of dawn asking me stupid questions."

"Sorry. Where's Eddie?"

"He had a meeting with the Prince. Don't say nothing to nobody about it. If they knew he left in the middle of the night, they'd give his bed to someone else. So just shut up and let me sleep." Jesse lies back down and covers his head with the blanket.

"You want some coffee? They brought out some coffee."

Jesse sits back up and stares at Larry again with menacing eyes. "Seriously? You're like a kid. You want some coffee? Go get you some coffee. Me? I wanna sleep some more, which means you need to shut up."

Banjo Larry is trying to be more personable lately, realizing he really doesn't have any real friends other than Eddie Fred. Prior to making this personal goal, Larry had been hesitant to come to the shelter and chose instead to brave the cold outside. He hated to ask for help, figuring also that if he took a cot, there would be one less bed available for someone who didn't choose to be out on the streets..

Many homeless shelters are run by church organizations whose volunteers hand out religious pamphlets and insist on hearing your sad story, whether you want to tell it or not. The only reason Larry gave in to Eddie and went to the shelter was because a few nights ago, a police officer made Banjo Larry get off the bench and out of the park. I was the same cop he had met when he first came to Santa Cruz in the summer time.

"Still haven't found your car, huh?" the grinning cop said to him. "Well, you should've looked harder, because you need to find someplace else to sleep tonight. The park's off-limits."

Larry spent the rest of the night wandering around, not allowed to sleep on a public bench and afraid to go anywhere deep enough to be out of the sight of the cops. He walked the trails of the park until three dunk college-aged kids caught up to Larry and beat him up, ripping off the strings and stomping a hole through the back of the guitar. After one of the guys pushed Larry to the ground mercilessly, Larry pulled a pocket knife from his jeans. The small knife was simply a tool before, but now it was a weapon of self-defense.

"All I want is for you to leave me alone," he pleaded to his attackers. "You got my guitar and that's all that I have. Just please leave me alone."

"What in the bag, you bum?"

"There's nothing in my bag. Just please leave me alone."

"You got a couple cans of pork n' beans in there? Some vodka and dirty socks?" one taunted him. "Gimme the bag, you bum."

"I don't want to use this knife on you, kid. Just please leave me alone."

The guy with the guitar bashed Larry over the head with it and as their victim stumbled back, another of the attackers hit the knife from Larry's hand. Then all three men began punching Larry until the helpless hobo fell to the ground in the fetal position, trying his damnedest to block himself from their kicks. One of the drunkards then grabbed the red backpack and tried to break it free of Banjo Larry's grasp.

"No!"

But the strap came loose from Larry's fingers and the attacker toppled backward to the ground with the bag. Larry immediately jumped forward onto the guy's chest and proceeded to punch him in the face until it was cut and bloody. He received a kick to his ribs and spun around to face another guy, who was by then in a boxing position in front of the homeless man. Like muscle memory, Larry snapped into the position he learned while boxing in high school and exchanged punches with the guy, who was joined by the third man while the first stayed sprawled on the ground moaning.

With both men hitting him from both sides, Larry fought back, hitting one of them particularly hard. The man went down, only to return with the red backpack.

"You want your bag, you bum? Go get it!" he laughed as he flung the bag into a grouping of bushes. Larry, unable to control his anger any longer, beat the two standing men bloody, pounding on them until their limp bodies lay flimsy like cloth dolls. He stood over the three hurt college kids, each of them probably close to ten years his junior, and each unawake yet motionless.

Fearing what would happen if that cop from earlier made his way back there, Banjo Larry picked his red backpack out of the bushes and slung it across his back. He retrieved his busted guitar and walked calmly away, wiping the blood from his eyes onto his sleeve.

It took him an hour of walking through the cold, but he finally made it to where Eddie had told him the shelter was. The people there said that there were no more beds and they're not allowed to take in any more people than they have cots for. They told him they'd call for an ambulance and get Larry to the hospital to fix up his face.

"No, thank you," he replied. "It's really not as bad as it looks."

They insisted on making the call, so Larry quickly walked away and curled up next to a dumpster in the alley behind the shelter. Cold, tired and afraid of sleeping in the alley, he stayed awake all night, wincing at the pain of his cut and swollen face.

The next morning, he was allowed to enter the shelter to find Eddie Fred and get some coffee and day-old donuts. Later on, he was given one of the empty cots and decided to stay for as long as they'd let him, out of the cold and away from drunk college kids.

But now, three days later, Eddie Fred is gone and Larry's face is less swollen and less bruised. He pours himself a cup of hot black coffee from the dispenser and is on his way back to his cot when he hears a sweet but concerned voice.

"Jesus, Larry. What happened to you?" Larry turns around to see Virginia in crisp green medical scrubs.

"Hey, what are you doing here?" he asks.

"I volunteered to help administer flu shots," she tells him. "What happened to your face?"

"Some guys tried to steal my stuff a few days ago. It's not as bad as it looks, really. They busted up my guitar, though."

"A few days ago? That looks fresh. Did you get it checked out?"

"There was a nurse here who looked me over the other day. I didn't need stitches. I iced it for the swelling, but it's just some bruising that's going away."

"Well, you look terrible, honestly. You could've been killed, Larry, and all over a guitar and backpack. You *still* got that money in there? That's not safe, Larry. Why don't you spend it on an apartment and some new clothes?"

"Because I don't want an apartment and some new clothes."

"You're an idiot, Larry," she says jokingly before jabbing him quickly in his arm with a syringe.

"What the hell!"

"Flu shot."

"I don't want a flu shot!"

"You don't know what you want. You're an idiot," again playfully. "Now go get some juice, Larry. You need vitamins."

"I don't want any juice."

"Again, Larry, you're an idiot, and you don't know what you want. And get a doughnut while you're at it. You're looking thin."

"Maybe I want to be thin," he argues.

"How many times do I have to tell you this, Larry?"

"Yeah, I'm an idiot," he finally agrees.

"And you don't know what you want," she smiles. "By the way, you should come over for dinner sometime. I'm a decent cook — well, I'm better than the folks here in the soup kitchen, at least."

"Eh, I don't know."

"Idiot," she reminded him. "You *do* want to come over for dinner. Do I really have to go over this with you again?"

Larry looks her in the eyes, which are warm and sincere.

"You really hurt my arm with that needle. You sure you're a real nurse. All you did was stab me. I could've done that myself."

Virginia grins at her friend while picking up a napkin and pen from the table and neatly writes her name and phone number on it, sounding out her name slowly as she writes it: Nurse Virginia Carnegie.

"I really hope you'll be staying here at the shelter for a while, at least until the winter is through. I know it's not luxury, but it has to be better than out there." She hands Larry the napkin, which he studies for several seconds. "I work days, mostly, but I'm free just about every night. I really want you to call me, Larry."

Larry folds the napkin neatly into a square and slides it into the pocket of his jeans. He looks back up to see her staring him seriously in the eyes.

"What?"

"Here's where you say, 'Yes, Virginia, I will call you soon.'"

"Yes, Virginia, I will call you soon," he repeats

verbatim.

"You'd better. Now get outta here and let me get back to work. I've got more people to stab in the arm."

NINETEEN

Banjo Larry knocks lightly on the door of Virginia's apartment, which the young woman opens up for him while smiling ecstatically for the clean-shaven gentleman in a freshly-pressed pair of trousers and button-down shirt.

"You really didn't have to walk all the way here, Larry," she says. "I could've easily gone out to get you."

"Nah, it wasn't too far," he says, "and, besides, I needed the exercise."

"All you get is exercise, Larry, with all that walking around that you do. You must be as strong as a horse. And you look very handsome, by the way."

Larry puts his red backpack down on the floor near the door of Virginia's apartment, along with his busted guitar. The instrument has been restrung — most likely improperly by Larry himself or Eddie Fred — and all of the holes, big or small, have been patched up with fresh duct tape.

"My god, Larry, why are you still carrying that old thing around?" Virginia asks while pointing to the guitar.

"Eh, it doesn't sound too much worse than it did before."

"Well, come here," she tells her dinner guest. "I want to give you something."

"Alright," he answers, following her around to the other side of her couch.

"I was gonna wrap it, but it's a strange shape and all." Virginia hands Larry a brand new guitar with a red bow stuck to the neck. "I have the little book it came with. I don't know a single thing about guitars, but according to the booklet, this particular guitar is an Ovation round back electric-acoustic, or something like that. The guy at the store said it's a good one. You can plug it in to a speaker thing, or you can just play it regular. So it's good for whatever you're doing with it, I guess."

"Jesus, Virginia. I think I saw this one in the store. These things are expensive."

"I'm making decent money now, thanks to you helping me pay for school and all." She's smiling, looking for his approval. "I got you something else, too. And you *have* to take 'em and you *have* to like 'em. I had a fashion-savvy young man help me pick them out."

As she hands Larry a stack of new clothes, her young son peeks over from behind the couch.

"I helped my mommy buy those," the little boy proudly brags. He's about five years old, it appears, right around the same age Ellis was when he died.

"And this is George," Virginia says, introducing her friend to her son.

"Well, thank you, George. These are really nice."

"They're thick," Virginia explains. "They should help keep you warm out there."

"Why do you live outside?" the little boy inquires aloud.

"Now, George, you hush," his mother warns. "Go wash your hands for dinner."

As George scurries off, Virginia says, "I washed them already to get all the starch out. I hate when new clothes are all stiff and uncomfortable like that when you first get 'em."

Larry puts the stack down next to his two guitars and the red backpack and sits down at the table.

"I lied about being a great cook," Virginia confesses. "But I do make pretty good lasagna if I follow the directions straight from the book."

"It sure smells good. It's been a while since I've had something home-cooked."

George joins Larry at the table as Virginia brings everyone their dinner plates with lasagna and hot, buttery corn.

"Do you say grace when you eat?" Virginia asks Banjo Larry.

"No, but I can."

"No, that's alright. We never do. I just wondered if you do. Well, dig in."

Larry waits for Virginia and George to start eating and then he begins. It's the best meal he can remember ever having.

"How is it?" Virginia asks. "You know, I was a damned good waitress, if I do say so myself, but it's not often I try my hand at being the cook. You know, by making things from scratch, I mean."

"It's better than how my mother made it, and she was a heck of a cook."

"It's probably just been a while since you've had a real meal. It's honestly not all that great. Is she still with us?"

"Who?"

"Your mother. Is she still with us?"

"Oh, you mean is she still alive. No, she passed on several years ago, when I was young." It's a boldfaced lie designed to change the subject, and he follows up with another just to solidify the topic switch. "Then my father died maybe ten years ago."

"That's a shame, Larry. Do you have anybody back home who might be missing you? What town was it that you're from again?"

"No, there's nobody back there looking for me," he answers one question while totally avoiding another. "I'm free and clear."

"You know, Larry, I don't understand why a man who appears college-educated and hands out thousands of dollars to complete strangers would choose to sleep out on the streets. That's for criminals and insane people, people who have no other options."

"Maybe I don't have any other options."

"Well, you're not insane and you don't seem like a criminal."

"Nobody ever questions me out there. I never have to explain myself to anybody."

"Point taken. No more prying." Virginia puts down her fork and looks away, apparently hurt by Larry's refusal to open up to her.

"No, that's not what I meant," he tries his best to explain. "Back before I came out here, I answered to people all the time — my boss, my parents …" He pauses for a few seconds before continuing, "… my wife and my son. I answered to people my whole life and they always expected something from me based on who I always had to be to them. Then I wandered outside one day and realized nobody expected anything out of me here because nobody knew who I was. Not even I knew who I was out here, so I had to sort of recreate myself from scratch."

"George, honey, are you finished?" The little boy nods to his mother. "Why don't you go watch some TV in your room? Just leave your plate and I'll take care of it."

Virginia waits for George to leave the room before she continues grilling Banjo Larry.

"What about your friends, Larry? Do you have any siblings? And why do I keep calling you Larry? What's your real name? Who are you?"

"My name is Banjo Larry and I live in the park. And I think I have to be getting home now."

"Larry, I'm sorry. Please don't go."

Larry stands up, politely wipes his mouth with his cloth napkin and puts it back down next to his plate.

"Thank you for dinner, Virginia. It really was the best meal I've had for as long as I can remember. And thank you for the guitar. It really was too much, but thank you for it just the same. I know Eddie will be thrilled when he sees it."

"At least let me give you a ride back, Larry." "No, it's alright, really," he insists. "It's a nice night out and I need the exercise."

"Will you at least come back sometime?" Virginia pleads with him. "I promise we won't talk about anything personal, just politics and religion."

Larry smiles. "Sure, Virginia."

"Are you going back to the shelter?"

"No, the weather's turning, so Eddie and I went back to the park. It's actually really nice out there."

"Well, at least put on those clothes I got you. I got 'em from an outdoor recreation store. They're supposed to be good for camping in, so they should keep you plenty warm out there."

"I will. They look nice."

Without any provocation by Larry, Virginia steps in and wraps her arms around Larry's neck, pulling him in for a hug. Banjo Larry is holding his belongings and can't quite hug her back, but he also doesn't resist. Virginia kisses him on the cheek then lets go, and Larry turns and walks away.

"You'd *better* call me soon, Larry."

TWENTY

Eddie Fred and Banjo Larry are sitting in the shade of a large, old tree, hiding from the heat of the California sun. The two men are admiring Larry's new guitar, which is tuned better than the old one could ever hold. Though he still can't play the guitar worth a damn, he's much more confident with the instrument now.

Willie Nelson's Dead, the halfwit recycler, rides his bike past the tree with his trash bags dangling from the handlebars, as per usual. He stops at some trash cans and begins to scavenge through them for recyclables.

Eddie yells the customary "Willie Nelson's Dead," to which he receives the expected reply of "Shut up!"

"No, you shut up!"

"Just leave him alone, Eddie," Larry scolds his childish friend.

"You know I don't usually mess with retarded folks, but that boy just irritates me sometimes."

"Just leave him alone." Larry starts to strum again on his guitar and Eddie yells at the guy again.

"Shut up!" he again is told.

"No, you shut up, spaceman!"

Willie Nelson's Dead jumps off his bike, quickly strips off his jacket, watch and trucker hat, then pounces on Eddie Fred before the old man has a chance to react. Eddie defends himself by slamming his attacker to the ground.

"I'm takin' your cans now as compensation for you hitting me," Eddie tells the guy. "Now you get on outta here before I really get to whoopin' on ya."

In a flash, Willie Nelson's Dead is back on his feet and somehow gets to choking Eddie from behind while simultaneously punching him in the back of the head and kneeing him in the spine. Larry yells at him to stop and Eddie tells Larry to *kill the sumbitch*. Larry grabs the guy around his ribcage and tries desperately to pull him off of his friend but is unable to break the man's grip of Eddie. Finally, and with much reluctance, Banjo Larry punches Willie Nelson's Dead in the side of the head. As the simpleton falls off of Eddie and rolls over onto his back, Larry kicks him in the ribs once to keep him from jumping back up again.

While Banjo Larry leans over the hurt man,

watching him to ensure there's no real damage, Eddie is already over at the trash cans, taking his enemy's bike with the two large bags of cans tied to the handlebars.

"Hurry up, man," Eddie yells back over his shoulder. "We gotta get outta here before that spaceman finds a cop."

"Leave it, Eddie."

"Hell no, Larry. That bastard owes me for this!"

"I said to *leave* it, Eddie. Put it *down*."

Eddie stops, turns around and stares at his belligerent partner.

"You're not a thief, Eddie," Larry continues. "You're better than that."

Eddie drops the bike and cans but doesn't budge further.

"He needs help, Eddie," Larry pleads. "He's hurt pretty bad."

"He's hurt?" Eddie exclaims in disbelief. "Man, I'm hurt. Come on!"

"He's hurt, Eddie."

"You do what you want, banjoman, but I'm outta here." Eddie continues walking away down the sidewalk away from the action.

Larry kneels over Willie Nelson's Dead to assess the man's condition. He removes a bottle of water from the small zippered pocket of his red backpack and pours some water into the injured man's mouth. The man drinks up the water eagerly and Larry knows he's alright.

"You need to get back on that bike over there and get home as fast as you can," Banjo Larry orders. "Have your mother make sure you're alright, but don't tell anybody else what happened out here. You hear me?"

As they both stand to their feet, Willie Nelson's Dead spits blood on the sidewalk.

"My tooth," the slow man groans. He shows Larry the tooth that he's holding in his hand. "And my ribs are broken."

"Damn," Larry mutters, knowing that this incident isn't quite over yet. "Alright, we have to get you to a doctor. Get your bike and come on. I'll carry your cans."

Larry walks him down the street, carrying not only his guitar while wearing his bag on his back, but he's also carrying the two enormous plastic bags of recyclables, putting every bit of strength he has into not letting anything drag the ground.

Upon arriving at the front of the hospital, Larry stands the bicycle at the bike rack and leans the bags of cans and bottles against it.

"But someone will steal it," the guy complains.

Larry removes one strap of his red backpack from his shoulder and brings the bag around to his chest. He unzips it partially and brings out a thick stack of bundled twenties, which he shoves into the man's jacket pocket.

"There," Larry tells Willie Nelson's Dead as he zips the man's pocket up around the money. "If your bike's gone when you get back, you can buy a new bike. And get a new jacket while you're at it. This one's been done for quite a while"

Larry walks the still whimpering man into the hospital and takes him directly to the front counter, telling the nurse there that he doesn't know the other man's name but that he was beaten in a park and he needs medical attention.

"Does he have an insurance card?" the unsympathetic the nurse asks.

"Probably not, but you're required by law to treat him. Ask your insurance questions later. Just get a doctor to take a look at him."

"Who are you, his lawyer?"

"No, but if you'd like my professional advice, don't mention Willie Nelson around that guy."

"Did Willie Nelson really beat this man up?" she asks, though nobody was going to answer her.

On his way out, Banjo Larry hears someone call his name and he turns around to see Virginia several yards down the main corridor, walking his way.

"Hey, what are you doing here?" she asks him. "I had to drop someone off, but I think he'll be okay. Is this your hospital? Those pink scrubs look good on you."

"Yeah, I'm enjoying it a lot more here than I ever liked working at the diner," Virginia says as she flashes that smile that Larry quietly swears brings him physical warmth whenever he sees it. "So far, I've mostly just changed out bedpans, given sponge baths and occasionally placed a catheter, but it's better than refilling coffee cups and scraping scraps of scrambled eggs into the trash can."

"I'm glad you're doing well," he tells her sincerely, "but, I've got to go find Eddie."

"Did Eddie beat up that man over there?"

"No, not exactly. But I have to make sure Eddie's alright."

"You wanna come over again, Larry? Have some dinner?"

"I thought you didn't want to be a waitress anymore," Larry grins at her while walking away backward toward the main doors, still facing his pretty friend.

"Seriously, Larry, give me a call sometime."

"I will, I promise." Larry walks out and Virginia goes back to work.

She goes over to check on Willie Nelson's Dead, who by now is sitting alone in a small room wearing only his underwear and t-shirt.

"Whoa, who told you to strip down?" she asks confused

"They always tell me to strip down," he answers, "every single time."

"Okay, then. I'm just gonna take your vitals," she tells him as she puts the cuff around his arm to check his blood pressure. "My name's Nurse Virginia. What's your name?"

"Leave me alone."

"And how old are you, sir?"

"Shut up."

"Very good, sir," Virginia humors the angry patient as she makes her way over to a chair where his clothes sit folded neatly. "Do you have an ID card, maybe a driver's license?"

She feels his pants and doesn't find a wallet, then picks his jacket off the back of the chair.

"No, that's my coat," the patient whines.

She searches around and feels something in the pocket, which she unzips to reveal the stack of cash.

"That's mine! Put that back!"

Surprised, she stuffs the money back into the jacket pocket and zips it up quickly.

"Jesus Christ, Larry."

TWENTY-ONE

For someone with just a little bit of sense — and a little bit of cents — finding a meal isn't really all that tough out on the streets.

The sidewalk food vendors are cheap and can even be considered affordable to a man with no solid income. In less than a few hours of playing in the warmer seasons, any ole busker can easily earn himself enough change for one of those big soft pretzels, a hot dog, or maybe even a cheeseburger. And for just a little bit more, he can buy himself an ice-cold can of soda to wash his meal down with.

The outside elements in a place like Santa Cruz aren't really all that tough to live in, even with the humidity. When it's sunny, you seek shade. When you're thirsty, you drink some water. When it's cold out, you try to get inside whenever possible. It's all basically just common sense involved, the same as with anybody else in this world, but maybe with a little bit more primitive creativity behind it.

When Banjo Larry has some extra change — or when nobody he knows can see him withdraw funds from his stash — he likes to splurge on his meals, even the simple ones. For example, he may get some bacon on his burger or some cheese dipping sauce for his pretzel. But his favorite, by far, is the bacon-wrapped, deep-fried hotdogs from one of the Mexican vendors. Then, like the cherry and hot fudge on top of an ice-cream sundae, the hotdog is covered in melted nacho cheese and sprinkled with sliced jalapenos. But, again, that's a delicacy reserved only for when his performances earn him extra change or when Eddie Fred is across town and out of sight.

And there are things a street person gets used to that the average individual never would. Take, for instance, the streams of sweat that will always be seen dripping down Banjo Larry's face in the summer time. It's simply pointless to wipe it away. And the flies nibbling here and there on the hotdog are more than tolerable. If they're swatted away, they'll just come back again. The wiser plan of action is to simply eat the food as quickly as possible to avoid the insects. But, no matter how long one has been outdoors, there's just no getting used to the flies crawling across a man's skin.

It's pointless to swat them away, yes, but it's a

natural habit to do so. And no matter how many times they're made to leave, they always return in a matter of seconds, and they always bring friends. They tickle the flesh and they nestle themselves into the beard and hair. They can frustrate a person enough to make him curse out loud, but the critters will never let up. A lot of times, Larry has noticed on his own, when a crazy or delusional man is talking to himself, he's usually just damning the flies to Hell. And you can't really fault a man for cursing the bugs that try to make a home for themselves within his ear canals and up his pant legs.

For the most part, Banjo Larry tries his best to ignore the sweat, the thirst and the accumulation of grime on his skin. But, unlike some of his more patient fellow hobos, he refuses to share his meal with a damned insect, especially his nacho cheese-smothered, sliced jalapeno-covered, deep-fried, bacon-wrapped hotdog and root beer.

TWENTY-TWO

It's cold outside now, not what people usually think of when they imagine the beach in California. But it feels like Alaska here, maybe even Antarctica, and nobody is comfortable with being outside for any extended period of time during this awful season.

The homeless, used to finding warmth the rest of the year, break down and move indoors to any shelter that has available space, some graciously taking any handouts when they are usually too proud to take more than a bit of spare change in exchange for a crudely played song on a damp street corner.

Folks blessed enough to have a permanent roof over their head also get outside less often, choosing instead to affix themselves to their couches behind a glowing box broadcasting reruns of programs they know they've already seen and corny holiday specials with the required happy endings. And since these good neighbors are inside their homes more, they're out among the street people less, which equates to fewer discarded coins in upside-down fedoras lying at the feet of would-be musicians, and even less motivation for the urchins to remain unnecessarily outdoors in the cold.

Banjo Larry and Eddie Fred are indoors once again, sitting on their respective cots inside a charity-run homeless shelter. The food here isn't much, but it's enough, and at least they don't have to pay for it. Fresh fruit is also more plentiful here than when they must hunt for their own meals, and right now Eddie and Larry are chomping into a pair of large red donated apples.

There are no real conversations here, everyone having already said everything they knew of to say quite some time ago. And within the confines of these warm walls, there are no new adventures to be had, and so no more inspiration for new conversations.

Larry, his mind wandering to more exciting recent memories, chuckles quietly to himself, though it's not below the range of Eddie Fred's hearing capabilities.

"What are you laughing at over there?" Eddie demands to know. "What the hell is so funny? If you got a joke, you don't keep it to yourself. Out with it, banjoman."

"No, it's not a joke, really," Larry explains.

"It's just something I said to Virginia the other day on Thanksgiving. You really should've come to that, Eddie. It was really good and there was definitely plenty."

"Never mind Thanksgiving dinner," Eddie argues. "Tell me what's so funny over there. I wanna hear it."

"It's nothing, really. You wouldn't find it funny, I swear."

"Damn, man," Eddie shakes his head in disappointment. "I never thought you was like that, man. Not you."

"What are talking about?"

"Prejudiced," Eddie lays out his claim. "Is it because I'm too old to get the joke? Is *that* it? I wouldn't understand your humor because I'm too old?"

"Oh, shut up, Eddie. You're not too old."

"Is it because I'm black then, you racist bastard?"

"How can I be racist, Eddie? You know I only have one real friend in this whole world, and he's black."

"Then tell me your young, white people joke."

"Alright then, but you aren't gonna think it's funny," Larry reminds him before starting the story. "So, Virginia was making pies for Thanksgiving."

"Okay, I'm following you so far."

"She was making one apple and the other one pumpkin, and she asked me what my favorite thing to put in a pie was. So I said …" He pauses for effect.

"Alright, and what did you say? Gimme the punch line, man."

"My teeth!" Larry delivers, grinning, to a silent one-man audience.

"Your teeth?" Eddie asks, shocked. "That's it?"

"Yeah, my teeth. I knew you wouldn't get it."

"Oh, I got it," Eddie insists, "but there just wasn't any humor in it — not enough to go laughing about it days later all by your lonesome. You young white people just don't know what's funny anymore."

"Well, Virginia laughed at it. But alright then," Banjo Larry counters, "you tell me a joke now. You show me what funny is."

"No, I ain't tellin' you no jokes because I ain't no comedian. I know my place in this world, and it ain't as no comedian."

"Then what is your place in this world, Eddie Fred?"

"As a wise old man," he responds. "God put me on this earth to be a wise old man. When I was your age, I was a wise old man. Twenty years before that, and even twenty years before that, I was a wise old man. I was born old and wise to teach young bucks like you how to get on in this world."

"Then why haven't you ever taught me anything?" Larry asks jokingly.

"Because you ain't never listened to what I'm teaching," Eddie replies with all seriousness. "You want me to teach you something right now, Banjo Larry?"

"Sure."

"Water," the old man says.

"Water," Larry repeats.

"Yeah, water. Drink as much of it as you can, wherever and whenever you can. It doesn't matter if it's hot outside or cold, you can never drink too much water."

"Water," Larry repeats again. "That's it?"

"Yeah, and make sure you pee regularly," the teacher continues. "There is such a thing as water poisoning. It's like overdosing on water or something, so you'd better pee it out just as often as you can."

"Yeah, you're funny, Eddie. A real comedian, alright."

"No, I'm just a wise old man, and you better start paying attention to me."

TWENTY-THREE

"Wake up, Larry. It's hotel day." Eddie Fred is rustling the limbs of a large bush Banjo Larry is trying in vain to continue sleeping under. "You got a few bucks?"

"We can't check in until eleven o'clock," Larry whines. "What time is it?"

"It's nine. Get up," Eddie demands. "I got some breakfast. Get up."

Larry crawls out from under the plant — which is actually a rather large grouping of these bushes — in the very center of the park. He joins his pal on a nearby bench and the two eat their warm burritos wrapped in thin foil and share a small plastic bottle of orange juice.

"Man, why do you still sleep in that bush? You're smack in the middle of the damn park."

"It's feels like a home," Larry smiles, "and nobody messes with me here."

"Yeah, well wait until you fall asleep and some bastard kids light that entire bush on fire. You're lucky all they did was kick your ass last time. Come on, get your stuff."

Larry picks up the red backpack, his guitar and a white plastic shopping bag with clean, folded clothes inside and he and Eddie take their time walking down the sidewalk toward the road. They have about eight miles to walk to get to the budget hotel, which is where they try to rent a room about once a week — when funds permits, of course. This is an easier task than one might imagine for a person of the street, as the hotel room is shared — commune-style — by usually half a dozen people, each taking their turn at the shower and washing their clothes in pay machines near the hotel office.

When they get to the hotel, they're met by a woman in the parking lot known as Mediterranean Heather.

"Where's Cricket?" she asks the men.

"Don't know. Ain't seen Cricket and Jesse for maybe two weeks," Eddie Fred tells her. "They said something about going to the city. Don't know how long they was planning to stay, though."

"Well, I ain't getting a room with you two," she balks. "I ain't settin' myself up to be raped tonight."

"What the hell are you even talking about, Heather? You've known Banjo Larry more than a year now and he ain't never said two words to you, good or bad. And you've also known me long enough to know that I'd never touch your nasty ass. Now gimme some damn money, both of you, and I'll go get us a room."

Larry and Heather each pull out some cash and they hand it to Eddie Fred, who swaggers over to the hotel office.

"Why ain't you married, Larry?" Heather asks from out of nowhere.

Larry just shakes his head and turns to squint at the sun.

"Why don't you ever talk to me? Are you shy, or do you just not like women?"

"It's hot out here," he finally offers.

"You're finally gonna open up and have a conversation with me and all you could pull out was 'It's hot out here'?"

"I'm just sayin' summer came early this year."

"It's a season, honey," she replies. "It's comes the same time every year. It even comes pre-marked on calendars."

Larry gives a wry smile and squints again at the sun.

"Why, you silly son-of-a-bitch," she slaps him on the arm while Larry actually starts laughing, quietly but aloud. "We had this same exact conversation, word-for-word, probably six months ago. But you said, 'It's cold out here. Winter came early this year.'"

Larry laughs again and Heather joins him.

"Cut that crap out." Eddie Fred returns with the room key. "We're upstairs. Let's go."

After he opens the door, Eddie Fred goes directly toward the back of the room. "I'm getting my shower first before Larry uses up all the shampoo again. And don't you two get to laughing again while I'm gone. I don't trust it."

Larry snatches the remote control off the dresser and lays his guitar, white plastic shopping bag and red backpack on a chair. He sits on the lone bed with his back against the wall, clicks on the TV and begins flipping through the channels.

"Comfy?" Heather asks.

"You see," Larry answers her, "this is what I miss about home."

"What, *SpongeBob?*" Heather sits down on the bed, next to Larry, with her back also up against the wall.

"Yeah, *SpongeBob*, television, a bed, a shower, sitting around doing nothing all day with no worries."

"You got worries, Larry? Where are you from?"

"A bush in the park." Larry smiles and turns toward Heather for a reaction.

She leans over and kisses him on the lips. Larry immediately jumps up off the bed and wipes his mouth with his hand. Heather stands herself up at the opposite side of the bed, looking embarrassed.

"Damn, you have a girlfriend. I knew it," she

tells herself, trying to find reason for the rejection. "I don't know why I did that. I'm sorry, Larry."

"No, I don't have a girlfriend."

"Oh, damn, Larry," she continues apologetically. "I didn't mean nothing by it."

"It's okay, Heather, really. No harm done. Let's just forget it ever happened."

"Okay, Larry, I'm so sorry. Let's just watch the television."

Larry picks his guitar off the chair and sets it against a wall, then sits in the chair with his bags on his lap. Mediterranean Heather sits back on the bed where she was before and the two of them continue watching the television quietly, each wanting to change the channel from the mindless cartoons but not saying so because that would require breaking the comfortable silence that has taken the place of the previous moment's actions.

Eddie Fred finally gets out of the shower and comes out of the bathroom with a towel wrapped around his waist and a fresh shave on his cheeks and neck, which only accentuates his full mustache — one that probably would have also been out of place twenty years earlier.

"You're up, Larry," he declares. "I got a pack of razors on the sink. If we don't use them up soon, they'll get rusty, so help yourself. I left out my scissors, too, just in case you needed them."

Larry stands and takes his bags into the

bathroom and closes the door behind him. He looks in the mirror and doesn't even recognize the person he sees looking back. Never before had he let his hair get even a bit shaggy, and how it's past his shoulders — and filthy. He hasn't shaved completely for several months now and has only trimmed it periodically. But now he has a full beard that's long enough to grasp handfuls of. He picks up the scissors and begins to cut away handfuls of facial hair, then he trims closer and closer to his face until his beard is just a short, patchy mess.

He turns on the faucet and dips his head into the sink, running the water throughout his greasy hair. With his head still in the sink, Larry wrings out his hair and stands back, staring at his reflection. He picks up the comb and pulls it straight back through his hair. With the thin scissors, he does his best to cut his hair straight, just above his neck. Once he's satisfied with the haircut, he picks up all the hair clippings and tosses them into the trash can.

Larry starts the shower and the room fills with a thick steam. The water is far too hot, but a hot shower is at best a weekly occurrence, so he accepts the heat without adjustment and climbs in past the cheap shower curtain. The whole place was cheap, in fact, and in his past life, neither he nor Tracy would've been able to bring themselves to enter such a dingy hotel. But now this place is like a paradise compared to cold, hard park benches and itchy bug-infested shrubbery.

With the complimentary bar of soap, Banjo Larry lathers himself up. He's a lot less picky nowadays about his soap, and even of who has used the soap before him. He works the lather all over his body and rinses all the suds off. He picks up the small complimentary bottles of shampoo and conditioner, but they are already empty as Eddie Fred has obviously used it all. He once again picks up the bar of soap and thoroughly works the lather into his hair and onto his face. He then takes his wet washcloth and harshly scrubs his face, as if it's the first and last cleaning his face will ever receive in this lifetime.

Feeling a sense of relaxation and in no hurry to get back to watching cartoons, Larry stays in the shower and enjoys the hot water and steam massaging both his body and mind. He finally turns off the water and steps out of the shower to dry off. He then uses one of Eddie's disposable razors and a little travel-size can of cheap shaving cream to completely shave his face. After wiping away the shaving cream and looking into the mirror at the face he hasn't seen in a little more than two years, he pulls a clean button-down shirt and pair of pants from the plastic bag and dresses himself.

He stuffs his dirty clothes into the plastic bag and opens the bathroom door to the bedroom, which is now dark and quiet as the lights and television are turned off. Larry hears the moaning of Mediterranean Heather and in the glow from the bathroom light he sees Eddie Fred peek his head out from under the blanket.

"Hey, Larry," Eddie greets his friend. "You was taking a while in the shower there so me and Heather decided to take a nap."

Heather peaks her head out right next to Eddie's. "Ooh, you look nice, Larry," she says. "You have a date?"

"You gonna go call her, Larry?" Eddie Fred asks him. "She's a pretty girl, man. You don't get too many chances out here with pretty girls."

"Hey, what about me?" complains the promiscuous woman lying next to Eddie.

"You shut the hell up." Eddie pulls the covers over Heather's head before turning his attention back to Larry.

"No, I was just gonna do some laundry," Larry answers. "Where's your clothes?"

"Hey, thanks, man. They're in a pile down there on the floor, and there's a stack of quarters on the table there."

"And my clothes are down there on the floor next to Eddie's," Heather says as she pops her head back out from under the blanket. "That's if you don't mind? Thanks, Larry."

Larry gathers up everyone's clothes and stuffs them all into the plastic bag with his own, scoops up the quarters and opens the door to leave.

"You gonna call her, Larry?"

Larry turns back and peers at Eddie in the

darkness that's only broken by the sliver of sunlight cutting in through the opening of the door.

"I mean you're looking all pretty for once," Eddie continues. "I figured you might be on your way to calling her."

Without an answer for Eddie, Banjo Larry closes the door behind himself and stands for a moment outside, thinking about his next move until he hears Eddie and Heather talking in the room beyond the hotel door.

"Who's he calling?" the woman nosily asks.

"Nobody. Just some girl."

"Is she a whore?"

"No, she's a good girl, damn you," Eddie shoots back sharply. "But that boy's afraid of her. Don't know what she sees in him, but good for him, I say."

With that, Larry walks away along the balcony, following the stairs down until he makes his way to the laundry room. There, he dumps all the clothes into the washer, pulls a small bottle of laundry soap out of the plastic bag and dumps all the contents of it in. Then he sets the machine on the hottest setting and puts in his quarters to start the wash.

There are only two chairs in the tiny laundry room and Larry sits on one near another man in the other chair.

"Banjo Larry," the other man says abruptly. "I almost didn't recognize you there except for that red bag. How you doing?"

He's a thin wiry man with a thick mustache that wouldn't appear so thick on a man of healthier weight. If you look at his eyes, you can see his true age of maybe forty, but the quick glance most people afford him would show him in his sixties. He's polishing his old shoes, which does its part to help keep some water out.

"Hey, Gopher," Larry replies. "Who are you here with?"

"I'm flying solo tonight. The Prince gave me hotel money so I could stay by myself. I have to meet up with some fellers. I give 'em something, they give me something, I give it to the Prince. But I ain't supposed to talk about it, so I can't tell you nothing. Sorry."

"You sure it's a good idea to be working for that man, the Prince?"

"It ain't no big deal, Larry. Like I said, I give 'em something, they give me something, and I take that something back to the Prince."

"Then why doesn't the Prince just do it himself?"

"Hey, man, everyone needs to eat," Gopher tries to justify his work. "Prince gives me some pocket money and I can eat for a while."

"Just be careful, Gopher. I really don't trust the Prince very much."

"Yeah, Larry, I will."

Gopher hands Larry the shoe brush and Larry slips off his shoes. They're not as stylish as the shoes he first came to town wearing so long ago, but they're better suited for the outdoor weather than those expensive running shoes were. He bought them at the Army surplus store and had to dirty them up a bit so he could pass them off to Eddie as a thrift store buy. He takes the polish from Gopher and polishes them up nice.

A buzzer sounds on a drier and Gopher stands up and walks over to it. He removes all the clothes and stuffs them into a white plastic bag and walks back over to Larry, who puts the brush and polish tin into a small cloth bag and hands it back to Gopher.

"Be careful, Gopher."

"Yeah, I'll see you tomorrow, Larry. We'll get some breakfast."

Gopher walks out the door and Larry picks up some of the religious reading material left there by a Jehovah's Witnesses and he flips through the pages. Then he puts it back down, picks up his red backpack and also walks out the door.

Larry makes his way down the side of the hotel until he comes to a payphone. He pulls a wrinkled napkin out of the backpack's small pocket and dials the number written on the paper.

"Hey, it's Larry," he says into the receiver. "What are you doing tomorrow morning?"

After the phone call, Larry goes back to the laundry room and pulls his clothes out of the washer and puts them into the drier. Then he sits back down and tries once again to read the

Watchtower magazine sitting where he'd left it on the chair.

Before too long, Eddie Fred walks through the door and says Heather was taking a shower and wanted to know if her clothes were dry yet because she hadn't brought any clean ones with her. Larry tells him that they have a few more minutes in the drier before they'll be ready.

"Okay, man," Eddie says, turning back toward the door. "I'll see you back upstairs. I'm gonna go see if there's something on the History Channel."

"I called her."

Eddie stops and turns back. "You called her? So you two are still friends? I was beginning to think you might've messed things up with her by now."

"Yeah, I'm going to see her tomorrow. There's a band playing at the park."

"Yeah, Jay Lakin and the Black Sky. I remember them from last year. They do a good show," Eddie tells him. "Nobody ever wants to throw their change down to hear us jam when they can catch those guys playin' for free in the pavilion. I gotta go see the Prince tomorrow, anyhow. You find me after the show and let me know how it goes with the waitress."

"She's a nurse now," Larry corrects him.

"A nurse, you say? Good for her, man. You tell her I said I'm happy for her. She's a good girl, Larry. Don't mess things up with her."

"Yeah."

"Alright, I'm gonna go check out the television. I'll see you upstairs."

Larry leans back in his chair and waits until the buzzer sounds, then he gets up and removes all the clothes from the drier. He folds all of his and stuffs them into the plastic bag. Then he folds all of Eddie's and Heather's clothes and puts them into their own piles. He slings his red backpack over his shoulders, slips his left wrist through the handles of the plastic bag and carries the other clothes up the stairs and to the room.

He knocks on the locked door and Heather answers, wearing only a towel. Larry hands her all the clothes and walks into the hotel room.

"Thanks, Larry." She immediately drops her towel on the floor and starts to put on her underwear.

"Damn you, woman," Eddie scolds her. "Nobody wants to see that. Go do that in the other room."

"Now, Eddie Fred, you just shush!" She picks up her clothes and hurries off past Larry to the bathroom.

Eddie takes his stack of clean clothes and stuffs them into his duffel bag.

"Thanks for doing the laundry, banjoman," he says. "You watch out for that Heather. She ain't right."

"Yeah, I figured that much out for myself," he whispers to keep her from hearing his gossip.

"I got us some burgers and fries from the

place next door," Eddie tells him, pointing to the fast food sack on the dresser. Larry takes the food and sits down on the chair.

"Thanks, Eddie. I'll get lunch tomorrow."

"No, I owed you from before. Anything you wanna watch on the tube?"

"No. Whatever's on, I guess."

Eddie continues watching the History Channel and Heather eventually returns from the bathroom, fully clothed except for her shoes. She sits on the bed next to Eddie and watches the TV with him while Larry eats his dinner. After quietly finishing his meal, Larry grabs a blanket that has fallen off the foot of the bed, lies down on the floor between the bed and door and drifts off to sleep.

TWENTY-FOUR

Dreaming is not avoidable, at least not without heavy medications, of which Banjo Larry has never taken. So, whenever he closes his eyes, wherever he may be, Banjo Larry dreams.

Sometimes the man dreams of happier times and, once realizing he's in a dream, wishes to die immediately so that he will forever be stuck in that world. At other times, however, he awakens screaming, afraid to ever go back to sleep and wishing to die immediately to avoid ever dreaming again. Tonight, Banjo Larry's late night situation more closely resembles the latter scenario.

The date — not the date in which he lies there dreaming, mind you, but rather the date to which the dream has brought him — is the night Tracy, his soul mate in the previous lifetime, had called the emergency personnel out to the home she shared with her husband, Fabian, and their son, Ellis.

When Banjo Larry awakens, so to speak, in this dream, the house has yet to be swarmed by policemen and paramedics. In fact, Tracy has yet to even make the phone call and Ellis is not yet dead, but sleeping peacefully in his cozy bed.

And Banjo Larry is in that room, watching through Fabian's eyes as their five-year-old son snoozes beside him, the boy's sleep only possible with strong medicine as any waking moment is spent vomiting and crying.

"Such suffering," he hears a voice say. "If there was any way I could ease your pain, I would, even if it meant I had to spend the rest of eternity in Hell."

A pillow is slid down over Ellis's face, pressed hard against the boy's nose and mouth by someone's hand. Ellis doesn't struggle any, the drugs the boy took earlier making sure of it, and the pillow stays in place far longer than is necessary to commit the deed. When the pillow finally rises, Ellis is just as he was, sleeping peacefully, though with his fragile chest no longer lifting and dropping as it had prior.

Banjo Larry, still through another's point of vision, looks up to see Tracy standing beside the child's bed. She's holding the pillow now, which matches the bed's comforter in baby blue fabric with baseballs and bats patterned in, representations of a sport her son was destined to never have gotten a chance to play.

"My baby's dead," she states simply and without emotion, herself more of just a ghost now than an actual living woman. She leans in and kisses her dead son on his forehead.

Without taking her eyes off of Ellis — and without ever blinking, for that matter — Tracy backs out of the bedroom, the pillow still in her left hand, which she raises to her face before breathing in deeply, smelling Ellis on the pillowcase as she closes her eyes tightly. After lowering the pillow and finally exhaling, Tracy opens her blank eyes, turns to the left mechanically and disappears into the darkness of the hallway toward their bedroom.

TWENTY-FIVE

Banjo Larry is rudely woken up, confused, disoriented and unaware of what kind of beast is attacking him. Squinting against the thin rays of sunlight sneaking in past the flimsy curtains, Larry makes out the image of Mediterranean Heather climbing on top of him.

Before he's able to properly execute any defense, Heather straddles Larry, wraps her arms around his neck and kisses him on the mouth. By then, his natural reaction is to push her away with as much force as possible, a daunting task with both of his arms trapped under both the blanket and Heather's body weight.

"It's okay, Larry," she tries to assure him. "Just go with it."

"No!" Larry squirms and tries to free his arms, but Heather is persistent and she kisses him again on the mouth.

"What the hell?" Eddie Fred jumps out of the bed he had shared last night with Mediterranean Heather and grabs the woman from behind, lifting her into the air and tossing her onto the floor next to the door.

As she scrambles to get to her feet, Eddie shoves her bag into her hands, opens the door and tosses her out.

"You damned tramp!" He slams the door in her face.

"Come on, Eddie, open the door," she whines from outside.

"Get outta here, harlot!" Eddie turns to Larry, who is still figuring out what had just taken place. "I told you that woman wasn't no good."

Eddie Fred picks up Heather's shoes from the floor in front of him and launches them out the door at her.

"Damn!" He shuts the door quickly. "There's cops out there. We gotta go before that tramp tells the cops we raped her or something. She ain't above doing something like that."

Larry tosses the blanket onto the bed and quickly puts his shoes on. The two men emerge from the room as an ambulance pulls into the hotel parking lot with its lights and sirens off.

"Alright, Banjo Larry," Eddie says, shaking his friend's hand. "I gotta go turn in the key. You go find your girl at the park. I might meet up with you later."

When Larry gets to the park, it's already early

afternoon and there are several dozens of people gathered there with more still coming in. Some folks are roller-skating along the sidewalks, some are tossing around Frisbees, and all seem to be enjoying the summer weather with the cool ocean breeze cutting gently through the otherwise hot air.

Larry makes his way over to the gazebo where Jay Lakin and the Black Sky, a somewhat popular local band that had a few regional hits more than a decade ago, will be performing a free show soon. The grass around the gazebo is dotted by the blankets of many families who are sitting there waiting for the show to begin. Some of the children are sitting on their father's shoulders, others are eating ice-cream or running around in circles — each just doing what kids do during a carefree day such as this in the park.

"Larry?" Larry turns around to see Virginia and her son, now a small, chubby boy of about seven or eight years. "Wow, I didn't even recognize you," Virginia smiles. "Losing that beard really takes ten years off. If it wasn't for that red backpack and guitar, I would've kept on walking right past you. George is the one who recognized you first."

"Hey, George."

"Hi, Larry," the boy answers. "Are you gonna play your guitar today?"

"No, not me. Some others guy are playing today. I'm just here to watch. You guys hungry? I think I saw some hotdogs and things over there."

"We were just heading that way ourselves," Virginia tells him.

Larry buys a couple of hotdogs and a soda for each of the three and they find a cozy spot in the grass to sit while the band comes on to play.

"Do you know these guys?" Virginia asks Banjo Larry.

"No, not personally, but I heard they're really good. They do a lot of covers, but some of their own stuff, too."

George finishes up his lunch and begins to dance in front of them. Larry encourages the boy by clapping along to the music and Virginia joins him, egging George on and drawing attention to him from fellow concertgoers.

"I really like my job at the hospital, Larry," Virginia takes a break from clapping. "I'm doing pretty well with it, too."

"Yeah?"

"Yeah, it's actually the job I've been wanting to do since I was young, but I was never able to afford going to school for it."

"We're not going to talk about the money again, are we?"

"No, Larry. No money talk," she assures him. "I applied over at the children's hospital in San Francisco, but I haven't heard anything back from them."

"They're a good hospital," he says, no longer clapping along to the beat of the song. "Lots of nice folks work over there."

"Yeah, and I think I'd like living in San Francisco."

"Well, then I hope they offer you the job."

"Would you visit me over there if I get the job?"

"You don't need some bum like me following you around, all the way to San Francisco."

"Oh, shut up, Larry," she snaps, now staring him coldly in the eyes. "If I thought you really were just some bum, you think I would've given you my phone number back then? You think you would've met my son? I wouldn't go on a lunch date to a concert in the park with some bum. You're not a bum, Larry. You've got some personal issues that you need to work out on your own, and you're doing it in a way that I honestly don't understand, but you're no bum."

Larry looks back into Virginia's eyes, which are still gazing into his with a glossy sheen to indicate she may tear up soon.

"And why, exactly, are you here with me?" he questions her. "What's this fascination you seem to have with me?"

"It's because you're not a bum, and all the other guys I meet — from the surfers to the suits — are all nothing *but* bums, regardless of what they think of themselves or where they live. You're hiding a lot from me, and from yourself, and you're pretending to be Banjo Larry the wandering hobo when you know that's not at all the truth. But still, as you lie to yourself and to me about who you really are, when I look into your eyes, I still see honesty."

"There ain't no honesty with this man," Eddie Fred jokes as he plops down on the grass next to Larry. "This guy goes around pretending to be a banjo picker, but have you ever heard him pluck on those strings? He honestly ain't no banjo picker."

Without a word, Larry passes Eddie Fred his remaining hotdog, which Eddie takes without so much as a 'thank you' and starts to shove it into his mouth.

"Hello, Eddie," Virginia greets the crude but likable man. "You keeping Larry here out of trouble?"

"Doing my best, ma'am. You're looking lovely as usual."

"Why, thank you, Eddie. Always the gentleman."

"Well, I try, ma'am."

"Larry, I'd like for you to come over tonight for dinner," Virginia states as a matter of fact. "These hotdogs aren't suitable for every meal. You need to come over for a good home-cooked meal every now and then."

"You can't pass up on that, Larry," Eddie interjects himself into the conversation. "A good meal doesn't come by very often." Then, turning to Virginia, he says, "He'll be there, ma'am. I'll make sure of it."

"And of course you're invited, too, Eddie," she smiles. "There's certainly enough room for one more and we'd be honored to have you."

"Well, I thank you, ma'am. And I normally wouldn't pass up a dinner invitation, but I have to meet up with the Prince tonight, so I'll have to regrettably decline. But I really do appreciate the offer."

"Another time then?" she asks sincerely.

"Certainly, Miss Virginia. I'll be looking forward to it."

"I thought you had a meeting with the Prince this morning," Larry says, drawing Eddie's attention away from the pretty lady.

"Got cancelled. Something came up earlier this morning and he wasn't available, so I have to go see him later tonight."

"You be careful with that guy."

"Will do, banjoman." Eddie pats Larry on the shoulder as he climbs to his feet. "I'll catch you later on, man." He turns to Virginia and tips his hat. "Ma'am, it was surely nice to see you again. Take it easy, Master George. You folks have a wonderful evening."

Virginia smiles. "And a good day to you, Eddie."

Eddie walks away through the grass, past the concert audience and out of sight.

"I got a new dog, Larry," Virginia says after Eddie is gone. "A laso apso."

"Yeah? Is that one of those little dogs?"

"Yeah, he's tiny. His name's Arlo, like Arlo Guthrie. Do you like Arlo Guthrie, Larry?"

"A little, I guess."

"Larry, I don't want you walking all the way to my place tonight. I'm gonna drive you over there, straight from here."

"Yeah, okay."

"Come on, George, we're leaving now."

"We're going now?" Larry asks her.

"Yep. I wanna beat the traffic."

"Alright."

They walk to the parking lot together and Virginia pushes the button on her key ring, which beeps the horn of her car once.

"It's over there," she says.

They arrive at her car, which is a red late model Toyota Camry. It's not brand new, but it's pretty close.

"This is a nice car."

"Yeah, it's alright. My last car bit the dust when I was working at the diner. I had to walk everywhere, but not anymore."

"Yeah, I know how that feels."

"You don't realize how much you've had to rely on walking and public transportation until you get a car of your own. You really do feel free."

"Free as a bird," Larry smiles.

"No, not a bird, Larry," Virginia counters with a grin. "Free as a butterfly."

Larry gives her a questioning look, but doesn't

argue.

"Birds take their flight for granted," Virginia explains without prompting. "A butterfly remembers what it's like to have to crawl around on the ground with all the other little bugs. Butterflies have to earn their right to fly. Birds are born privileged."

After dinner, Virginia puts George to bed and tells Larry it's raining pretty hard outside. She offers Larry some wine and they sit on the couch, sipping it slowly while watching *The Candidate* on television.

Virginia is on one end of the couch while Larry is on the other, a gap of several feet between them. They both stare at the television without ever really talking, Larry waiting out the rain and Virginia struggling to find a way to make Larry open up and talk about himself. Eventually, halfway through the film, Virginia lays her head on Larry's lap and continues watching the movie.

Larry is slightly uncomfortable with her being there but also enjoys the bit of affection. Soon, Virginia falls asleep there with her head still on his lap and Larry doesn't move for fear of waking her up. Before long, Banjo Larry is also asleep.

Virginia wakes up a few hours later, turns off the television and gets a blanket from her room to drape over Larry for warmth. As she turns off the table lamp, she notices Larry's red backpack by the door. She picks it up quietly and takes it to her bedroom, where she carefully unzips it and looks through the contents while Larry is sleeping in the next room.

She stacks up all the bundles of money on the bed — she doesn't count it but it has to be several hundreds of thousands of dollars — and makes a small pile of the few newspaper clippings he has stashed away in his bag. Some, she realizes, are stories of his disappearance and of his supposed drowning, and even his obituary. She reads over the clippings and puts them back down.

She then pulls out a small metal container from the red backpack and looks it over curiously until she is startled by the possibilities of its contents. She stuffs it, the newspaper clippings and all the money back into the red backpack, trying her best to make it look as though nothing had been disturbed, and zips it back up.

She returns the bag to the spot next to the door from where she took it, turns off the remaining lights in the living room and kitchen, makes her way down the hall to her bedroom and climbs into bed.

TWENTY-SIX

Banjo Larry's nose is buried into page fourteen of a small paperback book, not a safe practice for anyone while walking down a city sidewalk in the middle of the evening. He's straining his eyes to see the words in the dim glow of the streetlights.

As always, there are hundreds of cars passing right by Larry each mile that he travels, but one in particular on this night is driven by someone who recognizes the solitary man. In fact, this driver not only knows who Banjo Larry is, he's been driving around this area of town looking specifically for the hobo.

The car, a plain looking white Honda Civic, slows down to a crawl and follows Larry closely, the driver tapping lightly on the horn a few times to get Larry's attention. But to Larry, being a man of the street like he is, the sound of the horn does not seem out of place and it is dismissed as ordinary ambient noise. The driver of the Honda, however, refuses to be ignored and he lays on the horn until Larry is forced to acknowledge it.

"What the hell are you reading there?" Eddie Fred yells out from the driver seat while Larry is turning to face him.

"*It's On The Road* by Jack Kerouac. Virginia gave it to me," Larry answers. "Where'd you get this car?"

"Get in."

Ignoring the fact that Eddie really hadn't answered his question at all and putting too much faith in the idea that his only friend wouldn't make him an accomplice to car theft, Larry walks around to the passenger side of the Honda and climbs in, passing his guitar over to the back seat and positioning his red backpack safely on the floor between his feet.

"Whose car is this?"

"I borrowed it. How was your dinner?" Eddie asks, effectively changing the subject for the time being. "Did you get you some more of that lasagna?"

"No, we had sandwiches. Big, big sandwiches. Like deli-style. You should've come, Eddie," Larry replies before changing the topic back. "Whose car is this?"

"I told you. I borrowed it. From a valet uptown."

"You stole it? I can't go to jail, Eddie," Larry squirms in his seat. "Let me out."

"I borrowed it and we'll have it back in Santa Cruz by tomorrow. We'll park it someplace uptown and nobody's going to jail for it. You dig?" It seems like such a reasonable plan, at least to Eddie.

"*Back* in Santa Cruz? Where are you going?"

"*We* are going to San Francisco, banjoman. You said you had some business up there, anyway. Two birds with one stone, you could say."

"Alright, Eddie, what bird will you be killing?"

"I got an errand to run for the Prince. He was gonna have Gopher do it, but he got himself shanked in that hotel the other night. Same one we was staying in. So now I gotta run his errand."

"Gopher's dead? Someone stabbed him?" Larry is genuinely startled now. "I don't want anything to do with this, Eddie. I told you I didn't want to get involved with the Prince. I'm not working for him. Let me out of the car, Eddie."

"No, I'm the one that told you that you don't wanna get involved with working for the Prince. I told you that. But don't you worry because I won't be having you come with me on this errand. And don't you go telling the Prince I let you tag along, or we're both in some trouble. He wants me to go alone."

"I'm not tagging along, you son-of-a-bitch. You kidnapped me!"

Eddie drives the car down the freeway at a brisk but legal speed, hoping to not attract any attention from any cops they might pass. As they roll into San Francisco, Eddie says, "I ain't got no business until the morning. What do you wanna do until then? We can crash in Golden Gate Park for the night, but we've got some time to kill until then."

"I really have no ideas, Eddie."

They drive around for a while with nowhere really to go. Clearly, Eddie enjoys the freedom associated with driving a car and not having to walk around, and he doesn't want to give it up just yet.

"Let me show you a game we used to play when we were kids," Eddie says, breaking the silence between the two men. "I'll go first, then you'll have a go at it."

"What game?"

"It's called No Brakes. The rules are you can slow down by letting up on the gas, but you can't touch the brakes. As soon as you touch the brakes, your turn is over. Whoever gets farther down the road during their turn before touching that brake pedal wins the game. Right here is the starting point. You count how many blocks I get down before I have to stop the car. And don't you cheat me, Larry."

Eddie begins slowly, and after several blocks of near-misses, they come to an intersection where a crash appears imminent if Eddie doesn't end his turn.

"Alright, Eddie. End of the road for you,"

Larry tells him, slightly afraid Eddie might actually take his turn at the game a little too far.

"I don't think so, banjoman." Eddie turns the car in a sharp left up Lombard Street.

"This is the wrong way, Eddie. You're gonna kill us!"

As the car weaves through and approaches the top of what bills itself as "the crookedest street in the world," the headlights of another car appear at the ridge coming down the red brick road at them. Eddie eases up on the gas but doesn't touch the brakes, as that would clearly end his turn. Both cars lay on their horns and Eddie finally stomps on the accelerator and drives up the curb on the side of the road, narrowly missing the other car, and running down some of the flowers and neatly-trimmed hedges adorning the roadway.

Once at the top of the hill, the speeding Honda literally jumps a foot into the air and crashes down onto Hyde Street, spins an uncontrolled circle in the intersection and comes to a rest with the engine off.

"How many blocks was that, Larry?" Eddie's obviously pleased with the distance he's received in the first round of No Brakes.

"You almost killed us! What the hell is wrong with you?"

"How many blocks was that?" Eddie asks again, looking oblivious to his friend's anger. "Here, it's your turn." Eddie climbs out of the car and walks around and opens Larry's door.

"I'm not playing, Eddie."

"Come on, man, it's your turn."

"I'm not playing, Eddie," Larry repeats. "I concede. You win. Let's go!"

"Come on, you're driving. The cops will be here any minute, so you'd better get to driving."

Larry reluctantly unbuckles his seatbelt and gets out of the car, moving around to sit in the driver seat. He restarts the car and hurries on down the road, not really knowing where's he's going but desperate to get as far away from Lombard Street as possible.

Getting lost on their journey to nowhere, they see three guys in their early twenties conversing on a street corner, though looking a bit suspicious while doing it. Eddie tells Larry to pull over so he could ask for directions back over to the Golden Gate Park area, which at least is where they'll need to be by tomorrow.

One man — the apparent ringleader of the little gang of harmless social misfits — says he'll not only give Eddie directions, but he'll also throw in a map of the city from out of his own vehicle's glove box if only he and Banjo Larry would assist them with a project first.

"Depends on the project," Eddie answers to the proposal. "I ain't gonna agree to nothin' unless I know what it is first."

The task, the man tells him, is liberating a street sign with the word DIP on it from its post just up the road using a wrench supplied by the group of men.

"Why the hell do you want with a DIP sign," Eddie asks curiously.

"To hang on the wall in my bedroom," the young man replies. "You gonna do it or not?"

Eddie asks them to sweeten the deal by throwing in ten dollars for gas, which the ringleader agrees to before handing Eddie the wrench through the open window of the stolen Honda. Then Larry slowly drives the car along the curb to a spot several feet away from the DIP sign. The plan, they figure out, is for Eddie to jump from the passenger seat, quickly remove the sign and thrown it into the trunk of the car before anybody sees them. Then they'll deliver the goods to the gang of geeks down the street, collect the money and map and then drive directly to Golden Gate Park.

"You ready to do this, banjoman?" Eddie asks, pumping himself up for the mission.

"Ready for what? I'm just gonna sit here."

Before Eddie puts the plan into motion, a man walks up to the car pushing a bicycle and asks them what time it is. Larry looks at the clock on the dashboard and tells him it's about eleven o'clock.

"Damn it all to hell," the guy says with grave disappointment. "I was supposed to meet my kids about an hour ago but my bike got a flat."

"Yeah," Eddie tells him. "Things are tough all

over."

"Hey," the bicyclist says, looking into the back seat of the Honda. "What are you two fellas up to? Are ya busy?"

"We sure are," Eddie replies.

"Oh," the guy continues, anyway. "Because, you see, I was just gonna ask you guys if you could help me out with somethin' here. You see, since it's so late and all, I was just gonna ask you if you wouldn't mind ridin' with me over to where my kids are waitin' for me. It's just up the road. And maybe you could give my kids a ride to my house, since it's so late at night. That way they wouldn't have to walk all the way home. Beacause, it's really late, you see."

"Absolutely not," Eddie answers bluntly.

"Awe, come on, Eddie," Larry counters. "It's late. Those kids don't need to be walking around the city this late at night."

"Damn you, banjoman," Eddie says annoyed before turning back to the man standing next to his window. "I'll make you a deal. If you give us ten dollars for gas and remove that DIP sign with this here wrench, we'll give your damn kids a ride home. Deal?"

"Why do you want a DIP sign?"

"To hang on the wall in my bedroom. You gonna do it or not?"

The guy looks through his wallet and says that all he has is eight dollars, which Eddie takes from him while passing off the wrench.

The man leans his bike against the signpost and stands on top of it. Using the wrench, he takes out the top bolt and the sign spins around to hang upside down. He throws the two men in the car a thumbs-up and climbs off his bike. Just as he begins to loosen the bottom bolt, a police car pulls up and a cop gets out, shining his flashlight onto the man with the wrench.

"Just what are you doing there?"

"I was just fixing this here DIP sign because it was falling off."

"No, I just drove by here a minute ago and that sign wasn't falling off," the policeman tells him. "You know that's stealing city property, don't you?"

"Yes, sir. But I'll put it back up and we'll call it even, okay?"

"I don't think so, buddy. Put your hands behind your back."

The cop cuffs the guy without any resistance from the suspect and walks him back to the squad car. "Why do you want that DIP sign, anyway?"

"To hang on the wall in my bedroom."

As he's stuffed into the back of the police car, the man looks over at Eddie and silently mouths, "My kids. Get my kids."

Eddie nods and sinks down into the seat. The cop takes the bike and puts it into the trunk, using a bungee cord to keep the trunk lid down. Once the cruiser drives away, Larry and Eddie sit back up in their seats and start the car without saying a word.

They drive back to the young men and tell them that they couldn't get the sign because a cop came and arrested an associate of theirs who was contracted out to do the work for them.

"The sign is hanging there, easy to grab," Eddie tells them, "but the cop took the wrench with him."

"Well, you ain't getting the ten dollars now," the head geek sneers at them. "That wrench alone was worth more than ten dollars."

"Alright, just give us the map and we'll call it even."

One of the young men goes back to his car parked along the curb behind the Honda and returns with the map.

"Damn it, man," Eddie shouts. "This is a California map."

"Hello, old man, you're in California."

"This won't do me any good. I need a San Francisco map."

"Yeah, and I need a DIP sign for the wall in my bedroom, so we're even. Get outta here."

"No," insists Eddie. "You give me the ten dollars you owe me and then we'll call it even."

"Yeah, okay, I've got your ten dollars right here," one of the other guys says as he steps forward and pulls something out of his pocket, shoving it into Eddie's face.

As the man attempts to pull the trigger, Eddie

grabs at the end of the object and tries to wrestle it from the guy's fingers, but not before a shot is fired that could be heard blocks away in all directions.

The air horn — not a pistol, after all — comes free of the young man's grips while Larry slams on the gas pedal, screeching the tires in the escape while the geek is dragged down before rolling into the road.

"What the hell is that?" Larry screams, trying to remain in control of the speeding automobile.

"Some damn air horn, like they have on boats. I think I'm deaf now." Eddie drops the horn on the floor of the car and points over to the corner about a block ahead. "There's that guy's kids. Just keep driving past them."

"Come on, Eddie," his partner protests. "Their dad just got arrested for helping us out. The least we could do is uphold our end of the bargain and give them a ride home. It's late out."

"No, don't, Larry." But Larry pulls up to the curb even as Eddie warns him not to.

"Hey, kids," Eddie smiles at the kids after realizing he's helpless to get the car going again from the passenger seat. "Does your dad ride around on a bike?"

"Who are you?" the oldest boy asks.

"We're business associates of your dad. He's in jail, but we're supposed to give you a ride home."

"We're not going with you. Who the hell are you?"

"We know your dad. Just get in the car and tell us where your house is."

"Get lost. We're not going with you."

"Kids, let's not make this any harder than it has to be. Just get in the damn car."

"Get outta here, you perverts!" The oldest kid, probably in his early teens, throws a glass bottle at the car and it shatters the back door window.

"You little bastard," Eddie screams before the children launch more objects at the car, including a fast food soda cup that lands on Eddie's lap and explodes onto him.

Eddie opens the door and begins to climb out, but the oldest kid kicks the door closed onto Eddie's knee and reaches in through the open window, grabbing Eddie Fred's hair while trying to pull his head out. Banjo Larry reaches over and tries to pry the kid's fingers off of Eddie but can't. In desperation, Larry grabs the air horn and blasts it into the kid's face, which causes the boy to let go of the old man and stumble backward. Larry immediately slams the car into drive and they speed away.

"Damn it, Larry. Now I *know* I'm deaf! What the hell is wrong with people these days? Does everyone go around assaulting folks trying to lend a helping hand? We never should've stopped to help those bastards. And you need to start listening to me when I tell you these things!"

Larry continues driving, determined not to stop again but still not knowing where he's going.

"Hey, that's the Mitchell Brothers' place," Eddie exclaims excitedly. "I went there once in the seventy's. I thought it'd be closed down by now."

Larry continues driving forward, occasionally taking a left or right turn when he thinks it may take them in a more promising direction, which it never does.

"Turn here. Turn right here," Eddie commands, and Larry follows Eddie's directions. "Alright, stop the car."

Larry pulls the car over to the side of the road and parks.

"This is Haight-Ashbury." Eddie smiles, reminiscing about past times spent here.

"You know where we are?"

"You mean you don't? You're probably too young to remember none of this, but this place was happening many years back. It's dead now, but it was the *place* to be."

"So you *know* where we are?"

"Hell yeah, I know where we are. I can tell you all about the city. You wanna see where the Zodiac shot that cab driver? I know right where that corner's at. You wanna see it?"

"No, I wanna get to Golden Gate Park and out of this damned car."

"Alright, man. Let's get going then. Turn right here and I'll get us back to Golden Gate. You know, Larry, this air horn really saved our asses tonight. I'm keeping this thing on my person at all times."

As they drive, Eddie reaches back and starts knocking all the broken glass out of the back window.

"What are you doing, Eddie?"

"Getting all the window outta there. That way, it'll just look like the window's rolled down and it won't be so obvious that it's been busted."

As he finishes, he notices a man and a woman walking together down the road and he blasts the air horn at them, which frightens the couple immensely.

"Jesus Christ, Eddie. I almost crashed the car!"

"You see them jump? That was funny, man. I'm definitely keeping this thing on my person at all times."

As they approach another man on a bike, Eddie blasts him with the horn and the guy falls over, startled, which puts Eddie in a fit of laughter.

"Put it away, Eddie. You don't think the air horn will draw more attention to us in a stolen car than a broken window will? Put it away."

"Alright, man. Hey, you missed a turn."

"What turn? You never told me to turn."

"Well, pay attention next time. Flip a U-turn and go back that other way."

Larry cautiously makes the U-turn, driving back the way they came, and they see the man on the bike now lying on the ground with three other men beating him to a pulp. One of the attackers is pounding the man with a shoe, the other two with their fists. The three men run away as Honda pulls up and Larry and Eddie jump out to help the fallen man, who then pulls large knife.

"Hold up, fella," Eddie tries to calm the bloody man. "We're here to help you, man."

"Well, I don't need any help," he sputters. "And if I had just one more second with 'em, I would've killed them all!"

"They're gone now," Larry reassures him. "Come with us and we'll get you to a hospital."

"No, I'm alright," the guy says, spitting blood onto the sidewalk.

Not wanting to argue with the man, Eddie and Larry climb back into the car, with Eddie now in the driver seat, and they get back onto the road.

"That kinda crap really pisses me off," Eddie fumes. "You know what we're gonna do? We're gonna go find those bastards and beat their asses."

Larry protests, of course, but Eddie is driving the car now and won't stop. They cruise around and see two men standing and talking on the stoop of a townhouse.

"I recognize that dude's jacket," Eddie points to one of the men. "He's one of 'em!"

Eddie stomps on the brakes and the car screeches to a halt in front of the two men. Eddie jumps out first, and Larry reluctantly follows him, but only so he doesn't appear to abandon his only friend. Eddie grabs his suspect by the collar of his leather motorcycle jacket and proceeds to beat him down while the man's friend runs cowardly into the house. When Eddie Fred's opponent fights back in self-defense, Larry steps in to help Eddie — only the third time in his life that he has ever used his fists on someone in violence, and solidifying, at least in his own mind, his status as a bona fide man of the streets.

"Why, man?" the scared guy is screaming.

"For beating up that boy down the road," Eddie hastily explains between blows.

With Eddie Fred regaining complete control of the violent confrontation, Banjo Larry steps back down the stairs of the stoop onto the street. He checks both ways down the road for incoming cops or anybody else who might take the other guy's side in the fight after getting the wrong idea about Eddie's original selfless intentions.

"Man, I've been here all night," the bruised and partly bloody man pleads with his attacker.

Eddie stops punching the guy, releases the hold he has on the man's neck and looks hard at his face. He stands over the man, still glaring at him, then follows Banjo Larry down from the stoop to the sidewalk.

"Damn, Larry, them boys didn't have long hair like that," Eddie tells his partner in crime. "Damn it, man, get in the car."

Shaking his head but offering no apology, Eddie opens the driver side car door before turning back to address the man on the stoop, who is now struggling to sit up.

"You'd better be careful who you talk to out here," Eddie Fred warns him. "There's some dangerous folks about."

The homeless pair closes their doors and Eddie speeds the hot Honda down the road, slowing down only when he sees the flashing lights of a police car ahead. Two cops are at the scene of the earlier beat-down, taking a statement from the spastic man with the bicycle, who is still sitting on the curb with a bloody mouth and a missing shoe. Eddie and Larry stare in curiosity, as anybody else would, at the scene while they pass, then continue down the road toward Golden Gate Park.

They leave the car a few blocks away from the park, gathering all their belongings before walking down to the grass. The park is lit enough that they don't have to worry much about people messing with them while they sleep, and there are other homeless people around to act as added surveillance, just in case some bastard kids decide to start a round of Bum Burning in the middle of the night.

Banjo Larry and Eddie Fred find a couple of benches that back up to each other and haven't already been claimed by anybody else.

"It's late, man. Let's just get some sleep," Eddie tells Larry. "I have to go early tomorrow morning, so if I'm gone when you wake up, don't freak out. Just wait around here someplace and

I'll find you sometime tomorrow. But it might be late."

"I'll be here all day by myself? I don't know anything about this place. I don't know anybody out here."

"Well, make some friends then, maybe go sightseeing. Just don't play no music unless you know someone else don't already lay claim to that spot. People are real territorial out here. Just don't step on anybody's toes and you'll be alright."

TWENTY-SEVEN

Banjo Larry awakens on a bench, but not the sort of bench he's grown accustomed to waking up on. No, this one is different, in the same way that Fabian always felt out of place when first waking up in a hotel bed while on a business trip.

This bench is a bit softer than his usual style, as it's made of wood and metal, not simply the cheap, cold concrete in the park back home. This bench, the one with a little bit more give in the seat, is smack dab in the middle of San Francisco's Golden Gate Park. It's a big park, and it's scenic.

Larry sits up and takes in the view, which has changed considerably since the darkness of late last night.

"Wake up, Eddie," Larry calls out to the man sleeping on the bench behind him. "You're gonna be late."

There is no movement from the other bench, so Larry reaches over and nudges the snoozing lump, which still doesn't move. Larry pushes the heavy mass of blanket and man, which falls off the bench with a displeased grunt.

Standing up, Banjo Larry can now see that the sleeping man is not at all Eddie Fred, but a large, burly white guy with a red beard who reminds Larry of a television Viking.

"What the hell!" the Viking yells. "Who pushed me?"

"I don't know, man," Larry answers the scary giant. "It was some guy. He ran that way."

The Viking looks around. "What did he look like? You get a good look at him? I've got a knife and I'll stab that son-of-a-bitch right in the throat." He reaches his monstrous arm across the benches and puts his pointer finger to Larry's trachea. "Right there in the throat."

Feeling like a potential murder victim, Larry backs up away from the Viking's finger.

"No, I didn't get a good look at him. I just woke up."

"Well, I just went to sleep. I was up all night and if someone else wakes me up, I've got a knife and I'll stab them."

"Right in the throat?"

Nodding, the psychopath replies, "Right in the throat."

"Well, alright then," Banjo Larry smiles politely. "I have to take off now. You be careful, alright? You'll get a hell of a sunburn sleeping out here in the daytime."

"Yeah, alright. If you see that guy again, you let me know." He lies back down on his bench and pulls his little blanket over his head before again repeating, "Right in the throat."

Larry quickly stuffs his things back into his red backpack, picks up his guitar and hurries away. He crosses the street and enters an old-fashioned ice-cream shop where he asks the girl behind the counter if they serve coffee.

"You're looking for some coffee-flavored ice-cream?" the teenager asks.

"No, just a cup of coffee."

"Oh, well we just have ice-cream. Would you like some coffee-flavored ice-cream?"

"Is it any good?"

"I don't know, I guess so. I mean, it tastes like coffee."

"I see. Well, I'll take a single scoop of coffee-flavored ice-cream then. You have a restroom?"

The girl points to the back of the store and Larry heads back. Upon returning a few minutes later, he pays for his ice-cream and leaves his change in the tip jar.

When Larry exits the store eating his ice-cream, there's a silver man standing on a silver milk crate. The man appears to be a robot and as he moves, he's making mechanical-sounding noises with his mouth, ventriloquist-style. Below him is a small cardboard cigar box — also spray-painted silver — that he is using to collect change from people who may enjoy his robot performance.

Larry walks back across the street to the park and sits under a small, young tree to enjoy his ice-cream. Using his backpack as a sort of pillow, he tucks it behind his back as he rests up against the tree. His guitar is lying in front of him, just far enough away to avoid accidentally dropping any melted coffee-flavored ice-cream onto it.

"You know Soundgarden?" someone asks from above.

Larry looks up to see a twenty-something guy standing right in front of him. He's a muscular young man, dressed as you would probably expect a young man from San Francisco to dress, in flip-flop sandals, white shorts and a sky-blue polo shirt.

"Sound Garden? No, sorry. I'm not from around here. I don't know where anything is."

"No, they're from Seattle."

"Who is?"

"Soundgarden."

"Oh, well, I've never been to Seattle." Larry goes back to eating his ice-cream and the guy continues staring at him.

The young man's voice doesn't have a California accent — or California's complete lack of accent, depending on who you ask. The guy seems more Southern, but still not completely out of place in San Francisco.

"You're not from here, are you?" Larry finally asks the guy, who's obviously not going away any time soon.

"No, I'm on my way to Las Vegas from Louisiana. I got cheap tickets so now I have an all-day lay-over here in San Francisco. I got a cab and came out here to kill some time until my plane leaves late tonight."

"You going out there to gamble?"

"No, not really," the guy explains. "I'm meeting up with an old friend. We were actually in a band together many years ago. I was the drummer."

"Yeah, what was your name?"

"Hank Matthews."

"Your band's name was Hank Matthews?"

"No, the band's name was Vermont."

"Vermont?" Larry asks curiously. "Yeah, well I've never been to Vermont."

Hank grins, "Me neither."

"Were you famous?"

"No, but I'm related to someone famous — Loretta Young."

"Loretta Lynn? Yeah, I've heard of her," Larry tells the guy. "I grew up listening to her."

"No, Loretta Young," Hank corrects Banjo Larry. "She was an actress. I think she married Clark Gable, or maybe she just had a kid with him. Either way, she's famous and I'm related to her. Are you gonna play your guitar?"

"I hadn't planned on it. I'm eating my ice-cream cone for the time being," Larry explains to Hank. "And I'd hate to break it to you, man, but I'm not really much of a guitar player. A buddy of mine sings the songs and I just sort of strum along, pretending basically."

"You want me to teach you some Soundgarden? I can sing and you can strum along."

"That's awfully nice of you, but as soon as I finish this ice-cream cone, I've gotta go take care of some business across town."

"Yeah, alright," Hank says, disappointed. "I've got some things to see before I have to head back to the airport."

"It was nice meeting you, Hank. Good luck in Vegas."

Hank walks away while Larry finishes up his ice-cream, and once it's gone, Larry gets up and walks toward the direction of the city's piers. He continues down the sidewalk until he comes to a taxi cab unloading a passenger. As the woman gets out, Larry grabs the door, leans in and asks the driver if he knows where the children's hospital is.

"I'm pretty sure I do," he answers. "You got money?"

"Yeah."

"Get in."

Larry is driven right to the front of the children's hospital, a place he remembers none too fondly.

"Yeah, this is the place," he tells the driver before paying the fare and climbing out of the cab.

It's been a few years since he's been to this hospital, but the memories are still fresh in his mind. Not really knowing his next move, Larry walks over to a bench near the front of the hospital and sits down to consider his situation.

He watches people come and go, to and from the hospital. There are many parents, all looking like they haven't gotten nearly enough sleep lately, and Larry knows that he can sympathize with them. He occasionally sees a child accompany its parents into or out from the hospital, but not always. Some of the kids are obviously ill — thin and sometimes bald. Some of them are happy and laughing, possibly in recovery from whatever disease had ailed them — or possibly only at the beginning of their illness, not yet aware of the hell they will go through in the months or years to come, if they even live that long.

His concentration is broken, however, by his realization that someone is standing next to him and the smoke of this person's cigarette is circling Larry's head. Larry looks up to see a female doctor standing over him, looking down at him disapprovingly. She turns her head, then her entire body, away from him and toward the parking lot as soon as Larry's eyes meet with hers. She draws out another long drag from her cigarette, which is one of those extra-long ones stuck-up socialites usually smoke in movies.

Thinking her to be rude, Larry looks away from this uppity broad but soon realizes that with his red backpack and guitar both using a space, he had been taking up the entire bench.

"Oh, sorry about that," he apologizes as he picks up his backpack and places it on his lap, leans his guitar against the side of the bench and slides over to the end so the doctor would have plenty of room to sit. She looks over to him again, blows smoke in his direction and turns her head away once more, ignoring his polite gesture and apparently still refusing to sit next to the dirty bum.

"Point taken," he mumbles as he stands up, puts his backpack on and picks up his guitar. "I wouldn't want to sit next to me, neither."

He gets but a few steps away before she finally speaks. "Wait. Please stop."

Larry stops and turns around toward her. "You talking to me?"

"Yes, I'm sorry," she says to him. "I really didn't mean to offend you. I've just been having a rough morning and this is where I come to be alone for a few minutes. There's usually not anybody around here. Please sit. I'm sorry that I offended you. Please sit down."

Larry sits, his backpack still on his back and his guitar again at the side of the bench. The doctor sits at the other end of the bench and inhales another breath of smoke from her cigarette.

"Does my smoking bother you?" she asks sincerely. "This is the only place I'm allowed to smoke."

"No, it's fine. It doesn't bother me any."

"It's kind of ironic, don't you think? Here I am smoking a cigarette in between trying to save one child or another from cancer."

"I don't know about ironic," Banjo Larry answers. "Maybe hypocritical."

She smiles as she lets out a mouthful of smoke. "Yeah, hypocritical." She drops the cigarette between her feet and stamps it out. "I just had to tell the parents of a little girl that there's nothing more we can do for her and that she'll probably be dead before her next birthday. And now I'm expected to put on a fake smile and go talk to the parents of another little kid who probably won't see his next birthday. You wanna talk about hypocritical? All I can tell these parents is to just keep smiling and to live each and every day with a positive attitude. And then I come out here and cry because I know that there's not a damned thing in this world that can keep their kids from dying a slow, agonizing death, wilting away within their own bodies, shriveling up into nothing but miserable pain right in front of their eyes." She pulls out another cigarette and lights it up. "And here I go again."

"It's okay," Larry tells her calmly. "You're entitled."

"Thanks," she smiles through the tears, and after a couple of quick drags, she gives Larry a good look-over. "What are you doing here, playing for change?"

"No, actually, I was just sitting and remembering."

"Yeah, remembering what?"

"I used to take my son here for treatments. But that was a long time ago."

"How's he doing?"

"He's dead."

"Jesus, I'm sorry. I knew I shouldn't have asked, and then I went right ahead and put my foot in mouth again. I'm sorry."

"It's been a few years now. I was in town, so I thought I'd come by and reminisce, I guess."

"That's a hell of a thing to reminisce about," she tells him. "I'm sorry, but I didn't catch your name."

"It's Fabian," he answers, though it's not entirely the truth. "My life kinda went in a completely different direction after my son died, and sometimes it's good to reminisce — even about the bad things — just so I don't completely forget about all the good things, like who he was and who I was before."

"I suppose I understand," the lady doctor replies. "In my line of work, it seems I watch children die all the time, and so I feel a sense of personal failure when they don't beat their disease. Now, those are the children I think about most often — the ones who haunt me. But, really, if I wasn't here witnessing the children who don't beat the cancer, I also wouldn't be here to witness those who do."

"You need to start thinking about *those* kids more often, for your own sake."

"I know that, but it's easier said than done. I'm part of the senior staff, which means I also have to worry about the business side of it all, like doctor and nurse staffing, salaries, funding and all these other factors that help to remind me that it's a losing battle. As soon as one kid gets better, ten more get sick."

"What *about* the funding?"

"What do you mean."

"The hospital's funding, where does it come from?"

"Well, it's like most any other hospital, I suppose," she tells him. "We get money from the state and federal levels, and some from payments for procedures from insurance companies and some from fundraisers and some from private donations. Hospitals are really just big money pits, when you look at them from a business point-of-view."

"How does someone go about making a donation directly to the hospital?"

"What, someone like you? If you wanted to leave some money, I suppose all you'd have to do is walk in and put some change in one of the little boxes in there. They're on all the counters."

"What if it won't fit in the box? The cash, I mean. What if it won't fit in the little box?"

"Just how much cash are we talking about here?"

"If I give you some money, can I trust that it will get to where it needs to go, so that it could help pay for treatments and such for the kids?"

"I suppose," she answers, a bit puzzled, "but there are those boxes inside, and they're really not all that small. You could walk right in and slide it right into one of the boxes."

"Can you do it for me?"

Larry removes his backpack, opens the small pocket and pulls out a folded-up brown paper bag. He opens it and stands it on the bench between the doctor and himself. She watches him quietly and confused.

"Can you do this for me?" he asks her again.

"Well, I'd really rather not, to be completely honest with you."

Larry begins to unload his backpack of all of the cash, stacking the bundled twenty- and hundred-dollar bills neatly in the bag until it's about three-quarters full. He reaches into the top and slips a single twenty out, and then he rolls the top of the bag down. He looks up to the doctor, whose face is motionless and awestruck.

"Cab fare," he tells her, holding up the twenty. "I'd walk, but I have to get back pretty quickly."

He pockets the twenty-dollar bill and zips his red backpack up, then stands and slings the near-empty bag across his back and picks up his guitar.

"Can you take that in for me?" he asks her as he hands her the brown paper bag. "Can I trust that you'll get it to the right people? It's for the kids. It's to help you win a few more battles for them."

She simply stares at the bag in disbelief, so Larry places it in her lap.

"It's okay," he reassures her. "Take it inside."

She stands, now holding the bag in both arms. Freeing one hand, she removes the cigarette from her lips, tosses it to the cement and stamps it out with her shoe.

"Your break time is over, anyway," he smiles at her. "Can you take this in to the fundraising folks?"

"Yes, I'll get it to them," she tells him, still in a state of shock. "You can come with me. For this much money ..." She stops talking as people walk by, then continues when they're out of hearing range. "For this much money from a single donor, they'd probably name a wing of the hospital after you."

"But then it wouldn't be anonymous," Banjo Larry smiles. "You do it. Just make sure it goes to helping the kids."

She nods her head again and turns to walk away. After about a dozen steps, she turns back.

"Wait. I'm sorry," she calls to him, "but what was your name again?"

"Larry."

"Larry? Is that what you said it was before?"

"Banjo Larry," he clarifies.

"Banjo Larry?" she whispers quietly to herself before asking him, "Is that your real name?"

"It sure is," he answers, "but remember that it's supposed to be anonymous."

She nods again, smiles and then turns around to continue toward the hospital entrance, stopping just before entering and looking over to him once again. He nods to her this time and she smiles back, then returns the nod and continues in through the hospital doors. Once she has disappeared into the building, Larry turns and walks away, feeling as though a weight has been lifted off of his shoulders — both figuratively and literally.

When Larry arrives back at Golden Gate Park, he pays the cabbie and walks back across the grass toward the benches he and Eddie Fred slept on the night before. Eddie is sitting there with his back to Larry and Larry plops down on the bench next to his buddy.

"Hey, man," Eddie says to Banjo Larry. "Where the hell have you been all morning?"

"Sightseeing."

"You eat yet?"

"No," Banjo Larry replies.

"Come on then," Eddie says. "Let's go get some lunch. How much money do you have? We'll need to buy gas for the trip back to Santa Cruz."

"I'm almost out. We'll need to find a corner someplace and make some cash."

"You're almost out? Damn, Larry. You need to manage your money better. What have you been spending it on?"

"Just sightseeing."

TWENTY-EIGHT

"Check out what I can do," Banjo Larry says proudly to Eddie Fred as he thumbs the guitar strings in a pretty decent attempt at the intro to *Smoke On The Water*.

"Boy, what the hell is that?" Eddie asks, more annoyed than impressed.

"Deep Purple."

"It's deep something, alright. You goin' for the classics now, are ya? Why don't you try some Creedence?"

"I don't know any CCR."

"Come on," pressures the older man. "You just strum along, like duh, duh, duh, duh-duh, da-duh."

"*Down On The Corner?*"

"You know it, banjoman. We can be Willie and the Poor Boys."

"Isn't that a little cliché, Eddie?"

"How so?"

"Oh, come one, Eddie. A couple of hobos playing music on a street corner, one with a guitar and the other with a harp. You want to do exactly like the lyrics of the song and you don't find that at least a little cliché?"

"Take a look around you," Eddie replies. "You're homeless and you play music on the streets for money just to have a bite to eat. You tote around that damned bag everywhere you go, you sleep in a public park and you can count the change in a man's pocket just by hearing it jingle as he passes by. Your whole life is a cliché. Now pick up that banjo and pick me out some Creedence"

TWENTY-NINE

It's a calm and peaceful day here in Santa Cruz, the kind of day you wish every day would be like. There's a cool breeze blowing in lightly from the west, just skimming the top of the ocean and bringing with it inland only enough moisture to keep one's skin from drying out from the high sun, which seems bigger, brighter and simply more perfect today than usual.

The band of gypsies — made up of Banjo Larry, Eddie Fred, Jesse and Cricket — is once again jamming on a street corner in front of a small clothing boutique. Larry, now standing shoulder-to-shoulder with Eddie and no longer sitting hidden behind him, is strumming along on his guitar now with a lot more confidence and even a little bit more skill than ever before. Eddie, always the front man, is in his usual hunched-over position, blowing hard on his harmonica to an old blues tune while shuffling around in a bit of a dance that he correctly assumes would result in more change dropped into the turned-over fedora below him.

Larry takes a break from playing momentarily — though nobody really notices — to grasp Eddie's shoulder and pull him gently out of the path of the oncoming Tree Kicker. The crazed man runs by and Larry resumes his playing after a thank-you nod from Eddie, who never misses a musical beat.

The group plays into the early evening and after the final song, Jesse packs up his bongo drums into Cricket's cart.

"Well, we're shoving off now, boys," he says to Eddie and Larry. "Tomorrow's the big day and we need a good night's sleep."

"Well, good luck to you both, and it's about damned time," Eddie says to the couple. "I tell ya, Cricket, if Jesse wasn't gonna marry you pretty soon, I was gonna swoop on in and steal you from him."

"Yeah, Eddie, I believe you would've tried," Jesse grins to the old man.

"So you got a job and a place waiting for ya?" Larry asks.

"Yeah, Cricket's cousin Jasper got me a job and we'll be staying with them until we can scrape up enough for our own place."

"Well, you come back and see us every now and then," Eddie says to them. "Let us know how things are working out for you."

"We definitely will," Jesse promises before shaking this friends' hands while Cricket gives Eddie and Larry each a kiss on the cheek.

Then Jesse pushes the cart away with Cricket following her man into the darkness.

"Look over there," Eddie says, pointing down the block to where a man is rummaging through a trash can. "Willie Nelson's Dead."

"Just leave him alone, Eddie."

"I ain't gonna harass the boy. Haven't seen him in a while is all. Thought he might've packed up and moved or died or something. It's good to see him out and about again."

Eddie puts his harmonica to his lips and begins a tune with a more up-tempo pace, and Larry strums along the best he can. Soon, Eddie starts into the lyrics of *On The Road Again*.

Willie Nelson's Dead hears it, rides his shiny bicycle up to the front of the musicians and smiles. He reaches into his pants pocket — he now wears newer jeans that fit him right and a button-down shirt tucked neatly in — and pulls out a large handful of loose change, which he drops into the fedora at Eddie's feet. Eddie smiles, nods, and keeps singing. Willie Nelson's Dead smiles back and pedals his bike away, having just experienced a rare positive interaction with another human being.

Eddie Fred and Banjo Larry keep playing the song until it's finished, long after the man on the bike is out of sight into the night's darkness.

"You takin' requests tonight?" a woman's voice cuts through the air.

"Oh, hey, Dorothy."

"Hey, boys. You know any Frank Sinatra songs?" she smiles. "Ya know, I knew Frank back in the old days."

"Is that right, Dorothy?" Eddie humors her, finding it easier than starting an argument with the poor woman.

"Could've married him all those years ago," she brags, "but then things would've been different and I never would've had little Dave here."

Eddie looks down at the child, who is about six or seven years old now, and clearly a boy, no longer dressed up like a little girl.

"That's a handsome kid," Eddie says, smiling at Dorothy's son.

"Just like his daddy was," she returns. "Well, you boys have a good night. It's past his bedtime."

Eddie sits down on his crate as watches silently as Dorothy and her son walk away and disappear.

"Maybe that boy does have a chance at being normal," Eddie mutters to himself.

"Dorothy's cleaned herself up a bit, Eddie," Larry finally says.

"And I'm glad to see it," Eddie smiles as he takes a sip from his cup of hot coffee.

Three college-aged men, who all appear to be

heavily intoxicated, stagger around the building's corner and pause in front of Eddie and Larry.

"Play me a song, bums."

"We're on our break," Eddie tells the most vocal of the three men. "Come back later."

"Oh, come on. I'll pay you," the punk says, digging through the pocket of his blue jeans.

"Keep your damned money, kid," Eddie shakes his head disappointingly at the guy. "You probably need it more than we do."

The drunkard removes a handful of coins from his pocket and slams the change into the Styrofoam coffee cup Eddie is holding at his lap. The coffee splashes out all over Eddie's hands and legs and he drops the cup on the ground, the remainder of the coffee splashing onto the college kids' shoes.

"What the hell, bum!" the lead drunkard yells as he punches Eddie square in the nose, sending the poor man tumbling backward off of his crate.

Larry drops his guitar and receives a similar punch to his own face, and then another one to the back of his head. As he tries to regain his footing, he's hit again in the side of the skull and he falls over onto his side, where he feels the repeated kicks against his stomach, chest and head. Due to the excruciating pain, he finally blacks out.

Banjo Larry awakens some time later — probably just a matter of minutes or even just seconds — and he feels the terrible heat. He realizes the sleeves of his button-down shirt are on fire and he scrambles to get the top shirt off. Once removed, he throws his shirt to the ground and notices Eddie Fred lying on the ground motionless, all of his clothes set ablaze.

Larry immediately jumps onto his best friend, trying desperately to stop the fire. He manages to stamp out the fire on Eddie's pants, but the fire on his buddy's upper body just won't go out. Unable to get the clothing to cease burning, Larry claws at Eddie's thin windbreaker jacket, trying to rip it apart. The jacket's synthetic material is melting in Larry's hands and bonding to Eddie's t-shirt, but he finally gets most of it off of his friend's chest before Larry is once again overcome with dizziness and he falls over onto his back.

As the sirens and lights of the ambulance surround him, Banjo Larry loses consciousness and blacks out once again.

THIRTY

Nurse Virginia Carnegie rushes in through the hospital's front doors. She's not wearing her work uniform, but she is there concerned for the wellbeing of patients.

"Where is he, Sophie?" she asks another young nurse who is maybe in her very early twenties and also very thin and pretty.

"He's right down the hall," Nurse Sophie answers while popping up from her chair and rushing out from behind the desk area. "Here, he had this paper in his pocket. I saw your name and number and called you right away. Is he family?"

"Thanks, Sophie," Virginia says, taking the paper from her coworker. "How's he doing?"

"As far as I know, he's not too bad off. A couple of broken ribs, some scrapes and bruises. He hit his head pretty hard, but it doesn't look like a concussion. But his hands ..." Sophie pauses, as if waiting for Virginia to ask.

"What about his hands?"

"Somebody lit him on fire, Virginia. The rest of him is basically fine, but his hands are pretty bad, especially his fingers. He won't lose any of them, but they'll be in bandages for a while. No need for grafts, but still …"

Virginia is now at Larry's door. He's asleep with some bandages on his head and his entire hands wrapped up.

"Damn it, Larry," she whispers to herself.

"I know that, as far as the paperwork was concerned," Sophie starts, "they were wondering if you could maybe let them know some things about him, like his name and address. He didn't have any identification on him."

"He's a guitar player."

"Excuse me?" Sophie asks, confused.

"His fingers, how bad are they, really?"

"Oh, they'll be just fine once any infection's gone and the skin heals. He should eventually be able to use them just the same as before."

"He's a guitar player," Virginia repeats, this time a bit louder than before.

"Really? He looked homeless to me. Maybe he was just helping that other guy. I *know* he's homeless."

"What other guy?" Virginia demands. "Eddie?"

"Older black man? Kinda skinny and tall? You know him, too?"

"Yes, that's Eddie Fred. Where is he?"

"He's still in surgery," Sophie tells Virginia. "He's pretty bad. Are they friends of yours or something?"

"Sophie, what happened to Eddie?"

"He's still in surgery," Sophie says, not wanting to be the bearer of any terrible news. "I didn't get a good look at him."

"Damn it, Sophie," Virginia scolds. "You knew he was tall and skinny, damn it. You got a good enough look at him. Now tell me what's wrong with Eddie!"

"He got beat up pretty bad and they lit him on fire. When the EMTs showed up, the other guy — your friend, Larry, over there — was trying to put the fire out, but this Eddie guy was already burned up pretty bad."

Sophie stops talking and looks at Virginia, who is staring at Larry with tears running down both of her cheeks.

"Virginia, they found something strange in his bag. I was in there when they were looking through his bag for his identification. It was pretty creepy, actually."

"There's nothing in his bag that anybody here should be concerned with," Virginia snaps at the other young nurse. "It would be a good idea to just leave it alone."

"The cops are on their way," Sophie continues. "They said they'd be here soon."

"Did you call the cops because of what you

found in his bag? Whatever's in there is his and nobody else's. He hasn't broken any laws here."

"No, they just want to get statements so they can find the guys who did this to them," Sophie explains.

"You know the cops here don't care about the homeless. They'll never find the guys who did this. They won't even look."

"Virginia, if they didn't care, they wouldn't be coming here to take statements."

"Don't be so naïve, Sophie," Virginia says coldly. "Somebody called them, so now they have to come out to follow-up on it so they can file their report and close the case. It's just a formality. Where's their stuff?"

"Eddie went first because he was hurt worse, but your friend Larry was conscious when the EMTs put him into the second ambulance. He was yelling at them, saying he wasn't going anywhere without his things. So, to calm him down, one of the EMTs just grabbed everything he could find at the scene and shoved it into the ambulance with Larry."

"But where is it now, Sophie? As of this moment, where are all of their things?"

"It's on the floor there in a pile, on the other side of his bed," Sophie points into the room. "It's just his backpack and his guitar."

"That's everything he owns."

"Everything?"

"I'm gonna sit in here with Larry until he

wakes up. Can you go check on Eddie and let me know how he's doing?"

Sophie nods quietly and turns to leave. A few steps away, Virginia wants her to come back.

"Sophie," she calls out politely to the young nurse, who looks back into Larry's recovery room from the main hall. "Thank you."

Sophie once again nods quietly and walks away down the hall.

It is several hours later when Larry finally wakes up, and Virginia is asleep in the chair next to his bed.

"Where's my bag?" he calls out to nobody in particular, waking up his personal nurse. "Someone stole my bag."

"No, honey, it's right here," she calms him. "The paramedics brought it in. Your guitar's here, too."

"Where's Eddie?"

Virginia's eyes tear up again as Larry positions himself up in the bed.

"Virginia, where's Eddie?" the man asks again, his concern now obvious in his eyes.

"Larry, Eddie's dead," she tells him, running her fingers calmly through his matted hair. "I'm sorry, honey, but there was nothing more the doctors could do for him."

"Son-of-a-bitch," Banjo Larry mutters aloud, cupping the palms of his bandaged hands over his eyes.

"Larry, sweetie, Eddie never woke up," she

tries to comfort him as best as she possible can under the circumstances. "He didn't feel any of it, I promise. After he went unconscious out there, he just stayed asleep. He went very peacefully in his sleep and he didn't feel a thing."

"That's a damn lie and you know it," Larry says, his hands now away from his red, glossy eyes.

He looks away so Virginia can't see the tears rolling freely from the edges of his eyes, which he wipes away with the cloth on the back of his left hand. He slides back down in the bed until he's once again lying on his back.

"He was a ball of fire and I heard him screaming."

"Larry, you know I wouldn't lie to you. The police talked to a few other witnesses who saw it. Once Eddie went down, he never moved again. They think he was probably unconscious before any of the fire was even lit. He didn't feel any of it. I would never lie to you and you know it, dear."

"I heard the screaming."

"That was you, honey," she tells him through her own tears. "You were the one screaming while you were trying to put out the fire. That's how you burned your hands."

"There were witnesses?"

"Yes, and the police came here to get your statement but you were still sleeping."

"The cops were here?"

"Yes," she answers. "They said they'd be back later to talk to you. Does Eddie have any family?"

"Not that I know of. What's gonna happen to him?"

"A pauper's grave, I suppose, unless he has any family or friends who could pay for a burial."

"Well, I don't have any money, if that's what you're getting at."

"Awe, Larry, I knew that you carrying around all that cash was a bad idea," she sighs. "I knew it was gonna get you into some trouble sooner or later."

"Those punks weren't after the money, Virginia. I gave all that money away quite a while ago. Those kids were just out to hurt somebody and me and Eddie were just in the wrong place at the wrong time."

"Well, I'm glad you aren't carrying that money around anymore," she smiles. "Did it go to a good cause, at least? You hand it out to charity?"

"Something like that."

"Larry, why don't you come home with me?" she asks out of the blue. "I have plenty of space in my apartment and it has to be obvious to even you by now that living out on the streets just isn't a safe place for anybody."

"I just don't know if that's a good idea, Virginia."

"Then you don't have to stay forever," she pleads with him. "Just stay with me until your hands heal up. Come on, Larry. Hasn't this been enough of a wake- up call? You can't live outside anymore."

"I like it outside."

"Not all the time, Larry. You stayed in a hotel recently, probably the night before last."

Larry looks at her curiously, as if she's been spying on him. *How the hell did she know that?*

"You've got about a full day's worth of beard growth, I'd say," she explains to him. "Come home with me, Larry."

"I'm thirsty," he says, tired of the previous subject.

"Fine. Wait here. I'll go get you some ice water. Are you hungry?"

"No, just thirsty."

"You need to eat something," the nurse insists. "I'll find you something to eat. Just wait here, alright?"

Larry gives Virginia a cold, emotionless stare that sends a chill down the woman's spine, as if he was a different person than the man she had come to know in spurts over the past few years. When Virginia returns to Larry's room, he's fully clothed, his boots still untied with the laces tucked inside of them. He's unsuccessfully trying to refold the napkin with Virginia's name and number written on it, then gives up and slides the wrinkled paper into the small pocket of the backpack.

"Larry, sit down," Virginia demands. "What do you think you're doing?"

"I have to get outta here, Virginia."

"But why? Where are you going?"

Banjo Larry slings the red backpack over his shoulders, his hands still covered in the bandages but his head now unwrapped.

"Tell the people with the paperwork that I'm sorry, but I just don't have any insurance so I don't know who's gonna foot the bill for these wraps," he tells his nurse. "If it was up to me, I never would've come in here, but I was kinda taken by force."

Larry picks up his guitar by the end of the neck, his hand just barely able to get a good enough grip through the bandages.

"I'm sure I'll be seeing you around, Virginia. And if not, thank you for everything you've done for me. You're genuine. I only wish I could've known you when we were kids. Things could've turned out a whole lot differently for us."

Larry walks out the door of his room and continues on down the hall. Virginia, still holding onto the tray with the water pitcher, cookies and orange Jell-O, follows slowly behind him.

"Larry? Larry, please stop," she shouts down the corridor, but to no response. "Fabian?"

Larry stops and waits several seconds before turning around to face Virginia.

"You went through my bag?"

"I'm sorry, but I needed to know who you are, and you obviously weren't gonna tell me."

"I told you everything you needed to know.

You didn't have to go and conduct your own investigation."

"I know about your family," she tells her friend.

"You don't know anything about them."

"Because you never talk to me about them, Fabian."

"That's not my name!" he screams, the echo resonating off the walls of the long hallway. "My name is Banjo Larry and I play the guitar. And I'm going home now."

"I'm sorry, Larry," the woman cries. "Please stop."

"I'll see you around, Virginia." He's forcing a warm smile now. "Please give my best to George, won't ya?"

Larry turns and walks out the automatic doors while Virginia just stares as he goes. Once outside, he slips his backpack off of one shoulder and uses his teeth to unzip it.

"Still tucked in there safe," he mutters to himself. He pulls out Eddie's fedora, which someone must've stuffed in there not knowing which bum it belonged to. Larry knocks away the dust with the back side of his hand and lays the hat on top of his head. There's a taxi cab parked outside of the hospital and the driver is standing next to the car smoking a cigarette.

"How does it look?" Banjo Larry asks the cabbie.

"Looking sharp, my man," the driver humors

the hobo.

Banjo Larry smiles and continues on into his element, disappearing into the darkness.

THIRTY-ONE

No matter how comfortable you are with your predicament, or even with your expected future, you can never fully escape your past. The sooner you figure that out, the better off you'll be.

Banjo Larry, desperate to forge his new future, has become aware of this fact of life, and instead of trying to avoid certain memories, he's resolved to simply coexist with them — though it's really just one specific memory in particular.

This memory, which replays in his mind less often now than before but still more often than he's quite comfortable with, brings him back to Ellis's bedroom. And through the eyes of his former self, Banjo Larry watches his son sleep peacefully in his bed, the heavy medication the only reason the boney boy is not awake and crying.

"Such suffering," Banjo Larry's voice breaks

through the silence. "If there was any way I could ease your pain, I would, even if it meant I had to spend the rest of eternity in Hell."

Drops of tears roll down Ellis's cheeks, not from the sleeping boy, however, but from the father who stands leaning over his only son.

The man lifts his son's head slightly, gently sliding one of the boy's pillows out from under him, and then he hugs the pillow tightly against his own chest, sobbing uncontrollably. He places the pillow over Ellis's face and presses in firmly, making sure to completely cover the boy's nose and face area. When he's sure his son is dead, he lets go of the pillow, leaving it in place to hide the face of the dead boy.

"My baby's dead," Tracy speaks up from the foot of Ellis's bed. She moves in closer to her dead son, removing the pillow from his face. She, too, leans in to the boy, placing a loving kiss on Ellis's forehead.

Backing up to the doorway of her son's room, Tracy raises the pillow to her own face, inhales deeply, and then walks slowly down the hall toward her room.

Banjo Larry — though as a different man entirely in his dream — wipes the water from his eyes and carries himself clumsily down the stairs and out the front door of his home. He climbs into his car and maneuvers the machine backward out of his driveway, onto the roadway and down the residential street.

THIRTY-TWO

Banjo Larry's eyes snap open as he wakes up on the park bench. Running past him is a young woman and her chocolate-colored Labrador. Neither the woman nor the dog pays the homeless man any attention as they enjoy their early morning exercise.

Strolling down the sidewalk that cuts through the center of the public park, Banjo Larry smiles at a simpleton known only as Willie Nelson's Dead, who at this time is hunched over a trash can in which he's foraging for recyclables. The guy waves back at Larry, then drops an aluminum soda can into one of the large plastic bags he has tied to his bicycle's handlebars.

Still walking, Banjo Larry steps aside for the infamous Tree Kicker, who, as commanded by Larry, flies up into the air at a lower-hanging tree branch.

Upon reaching a water fountain at the side of the cement path, the wandering homeless man removes a plastic water bottle from his dirty red backpack and fills it up, takes a drink from it and fills it up again.

"Water," he says aloud to himself. "Drink as much of it as you can, wherever and whenever you can. You can never drink too much water."

His stomach not completely satisfied with a simple gulp of water, Larry makes his way to a sidewalk newspaper stand. There he buys a single candy bar, which he eats immediately, and after a brief but friendly confrontation by a man in a honking BMW, he has found himself out on the beach.

He stops at a trash can positioned conveniently in the sand and removes handfuls of small paper from the interior of his red backpack, most of which are wrinkled newspaper clippings. As he clears his bag of the unwanted cargo, he singles out a napkin with the name and telephone number of a certain nurse written on it. He holds it aside, and when everything else is gone, he tosses it back into the bag before zipping up the pocket again.

By the time Banjo Larry finally reaches the water, there are still very few people on the beach, even for a weekday morning. He continues walking for a while longer until he comes to what he considers to be the perfect place. He kneels just where the wet sand meets the dry sand, takes off his backpack again and removes a small metal container from the larger opening of the bag.

"I'm sorry I didn't get around to doing this sooner," he says aloud as he holds the urn in front of his chest. "I couldn't do it before, but I know it's time now."

He peels away at the black electrical tape securing the lid to the container, and once it's completely removed, he shoves the wad of tape into the red bag. With his backpack again in its proper place behind him, Banjo Larry walks slowly out into the water until it is knee-high. He watches the tide roll in a few times and before it has a chance to move back out again, Larry begins to dump the contents of the urn into the water beside him, making sure to scatter the ashes around evenly along the surface. The tide pulls the ashes out to the ocean, and soon they are mixed thoroughly into the waves, and Larry watches attentively to ensure they are all gone from sight.

The man then turns around and makes his way back toward dry land. Realizing he's still holding the urn in his right hand, Larry again faces the sea and reels back his arm to launch the metal canister far into the break of the largest wave.

Once back on the sand, Larry continues walking through the beach, through the small parking lot and onto the sidewalk along the street.

And Banjo Larry just keeps on walking.